Mere Appearances

A Samantha and Jacob Lowen Mystery

Jo,
You are in both
Categories listed on
page 4. Your encouragement
to write spurred me on —
Your friendship and wisdom still
inspires me.

James Stamoolis

4/25/2023

James J Stamoolis

"Stop judging by mere appearances, and make a right judgment."
The Gospel of John, Chapter 7 verse 24

For those who encouraged my writing efforts I gratefully dedicate this novel.

My debt to my mentors, instructors, friends and family is greater than I can relate.

Chapter One

"I should've been a cowboy. I should've learned to rope and ride" Jake sang along to Toby Keith's "Should have been a cowboy," on his CD player.

Entering the Jake's study, Samantha, Jake's wife couldn't resist the comment, "Jake, maybe should've been a cowboy, but a cowboy singer you are not."

"Thanks, Sam. I was just trying to get into the mood of living here in the west" as he looked up from the catalogue on his desk.

"Scottsdale, Arizona hardly qualifies as the wild west. Most of the residents are snowbirds."

"But Sam, we're on the edge of the desert and near so much history. Plus the brochure on the town makes a lot of the cowboy heritage."

"You can take the history professor out of the classroom, but not the history out of the professor."

"Well, I am switching my special field of interest from the Civil War to the West."

"That's just an excuse for you to buy more books and paraphernalia."

"True, but a good one."

Jake's collection of books and artifacts on the Civil War had accompanied them on their move from Illinois. Samantha, his wife of thirty-five years, was told by her doctors that unless they moved to a warmer and drier climate, her asthma would only get worse and more debilitating. An elementary school teacher for twenty five years, she was eligible for early retirement under the state's buyout provision. She missed the classroom interaction, but not the classroom management of increasingly unruly children. Their comfortable home in Scottsdale had sufficient room for Jake's library and enough extra bedrooms for their children and grandchildren to visit. A plus was the view of the Usery Mountains from the back of the home. Lovers of the great outdoors, Samantha and Jake found it particularly soothing to look out over their backyard and see such beauty.

"Anyway, Sam, I already have a collection of western guns; now I'm just into cowboy stuff more wholeheartedly. Just look at this catalogue that came in this morning's mail, it has lots of cool western wear."

"Jake, in all the years I've known you, you have always been into everything you do wholeheartedly. Whether it was sports cars, WWII history, the Civil War or now western lore."

"But Samantha, you know that I've no bad habits. I don't smoke or gamble and I'm a moderate drinker."

"Jake, you only call me Samantha when you want to get something out of me. What is it now?"

"Samantha, how can you say that?"

"Long experience, get to the point!"

"Okay. You know how I attended that Cowboy Shooting event? Well, to enter as a competitor I need to get some more equipment and …."

"What kind of equipment?"

"Well, I have almost all the right guns. Just a holster, a coach gun and some western wear."

"I suppose you have already figured out we can afford it." Since Jake's Civil War novels were selling well, this was perhaps a rhetorical question. It was his royalties that enabled them to pay cash for their current home and for him to take early retirement from his job as a professor of history.

"If you'd like to come with me, there are some great clothes for women in this catalogue. You would look great in them; it would show off your great figure and lovely legs." Jake knew that Samantha was secretly proud that she had kept her weight at 135 pounds which was curvaceously distributed on her 5'8" frame.

"Jacob Lowen, you are impossible!"

In spite of herself, she let Jake show her the clothes in the catalogue.

Chapter Two

The Lowens were settling into a routine. Most of the unpacking had already been done, with Jake's books overflowing his study and lining the walls of the guest rooms and the family room. His collection was well organized with each room featuring a particular subject. Samantha figured it would probably drive some of their overnight guest crazy only seeing books in the same field, but it worked for Jake's research. The stuff he used frequently was in his office and on the bookshelves that lined the halls just outside. Samantha wondered if when he started writing in a new area he would want to reorganize. This happened a couple of times in their home in Illinois, much to her consternation, as there were piles of books on the floor until Jake had his system perfected. She suppressed a shudder and hoped he was happy with the current arrangement. She thought she had caught him eyeing space and measuring walls for more bookcases but Jake denied it, though not very successfully.

Jake took Jasmine, their golden retriever for a walk every morning and evening. Often if he were stuck on a problem in his writing or if he felt the need to stretch his muscles, he would go out during the day with the dog for a hike. Usually Samantha accompanied him on these jaunts as they explored the nearby McDowell Sonoran Conservancy. It was great to have this park so near.

"Sam, I am going to hike in the McDowell Sonora Preserve. Feel up to coming with me?"

"Sorry, honey, my knee is acting up. Are you taking Jasmine?"

"Yeah, the exercise will do us both some good."

Fifteen minutes later having parked at the Bell Road access point, Jake and Jasmine were happily traversing the Levee Trail. Jake never tired of the views of the McDowell Mountains and the amazing flora and fauna of the desert.

"Flora and fauna, I even think like a professor, eh Jasmine?"

At the sound of her name, the dog looked up at Jake.

"Is this a great place to live or what? We couldn't be out like this back in Illinois, right girl?"

The only response from the dog was the wag of her tail. She was too intent on the smells that she was encountering on their walk.

"Too many smells, too little time, eh, Jas?"

The retriever only acknowledged hearing her nickname with a slight turn of her head and a lift of ears.

Jake continued his one sided conversation. "Wasn't as hard to leave college teaching and our home in Illinois as I feared it would be. We can get used to this life in the west. I was tired of teaching uncaring undergraduates. Working with grad students, while fun, but starting to lose its luster. Maybe I can get an adjunct post at the university if I get bored. Meanwhile I have my writing to do. This move has been great for me to finish work on those Civil War monographs and that novel my publisher is clamoring for is well under way. And Sam is so much better living out here, isn't she Jasmine?"

Again, the dog perked up at the sound of her name, but made no comment.

"That's one of your strong points, Jas. You're a good listener. Not much of a talker, but a great listener."

The rules of the preserve required dogs to be on a leash, which normally was not a problem for the retriever. This afternoon, however, Jasmine strained at the leash and let out a low growl.

"What's that, some dead animal you've caught a whiff of? Let's keep going."

But the retriever continued to growl and went into a point.

Jake turned his attention to the area where Jasmine was pointing. Just off the trail, Jake saw the bones of what appeared to be a human arm. The flesh was off the forearm and the radius showed signs of gnawing by an animal. Looking more closely, Jake saw the arm was protruding from a mound of dirt slightly off the trail. It appeared that the mound covered the rest of a body.

"Good girl, you've not forgotten your search and rescue training. This is not an ancient burial site but one that is fairly recent. Let's see if we have decent cell phone reception here."

Calling the sheriff's office, Jake identified their position and promised to wait till the deputy arrived and not touch anything.

"Mr. Lowen, I am Deputy Sheriff John Lodestone. Can you show me where you discovered the body?"

Deputy Lodestone was not your stereo typical policeman. If he had a predilection to coffee and donuts, then he must follow a rigorous workout schedule. As tall as Jake, he had at least twenty pounds on him, but it looked it was all muscle. Jake had the feeling that Lodestone had played football in college; he carried himself like a ballplayer.

Twenty minutes later, the deputy had taken Jake's statement and called for a crime scene unit to document the site and dig up the body. Receiving permission to stick around as long as Jasmine and he stayed out of the way, Jake had a ringside seat as the medical examiner's team disinterred the nude and partially decomposed body of a woman. The body had been preserved to some extent by the heat and dry climate.

"Tell me again how you found the body, Mr. Lowen?"

"Well, Jasmine and I trained in Illinois as a search and rescue team. We looked for survivors of tragedies. Our team was called in to search collapsed buildings. We also searched for people lost in the woods. My dog has a superior nose for cadavers and was one of the lead dogs of our group."

"Was that your full time occupation?"

"No, Deputy Lodestone, I was a college history professor. This was just volunteer service for me, but Jasmine took her work very seriously and once at a site wouldn't leave until we found what we were looking for. Very tenacious dog."

"Useful skill. Do you plan on volunteering now that you've moved out here?"

"I was thinking about joining the Arizona Rangers."

"What do you do now?"

"I retired. We moved out here for my wife's health."

"According to the date on your driver's license, you are only 58. Take an early retirement?"

"Matter of fact, I did. Wife's health was deteriorating, needed to move to a better climate, and here we are."

As the team from the medical examiner brought the body up, Deputy Lodestone indicated for them to stop. "In spite of the injury to her face, do you recognize her, Mr. Lowen?"

Looking at the body, Jake was stunned to see the woman's face bashed in. "'Fraid not. Don't think it's anyone I've seen before. But my wife and I only moved here about six weeks ago. But even then, there not much of her face left to identify."

"Have you walked this trail much?"

"Couple of times. Haven't been here for at least a week, maybe longer. I am trying out the trails in the preserve."

"She has been in the ground about two months, give or take a couple of weeks. The spring rains washed the dirt off the arm. Whoever buried her didn't bother to dig a deep hole. If you haven't been here for a while, it explains why your dog didn't find the body sooner."

"Jasmine had an injury to her paw about two weeks ago. I kept her off these trails and closer to home, now that I think about it, I was here without her about ten days ago taking photos."

"Do you remember photographing this area?"

"I'll check at home, but the couple of times I have walked here, I've not seen anyone off the trail. Someone dropping a body off here in daylight would be visible to anyone on the trail."

"You're right. Probably this was done at night. Thanks very much, Mr. Lowen. We will be in touch if we need anything else from you."

Walking back to the Jeep, Jake couldn't help saying to Jasmine. "Good work, gal. You were a hero today. Wait till Sam hears about our adventure."

But Jake's news would have to wait. As he walked into the hall, Samantha greeted him.

"Come meet our new neighbors, Jake. This is Harold and Cindy Rousseau. They live next door. I saw them and invited them in for a cool drink."

"Pleased to meet you both." Jake eyed his new neighbors.

Cindy looked in her late twenties or early thirties, tall, long legged, with shoulder length blond hair and sparking blue eyes. She was a real beauty. On the other hand, Harold looked older, in his fifties, maybe a little younger. He was stocky but in spite of his bulging waist, his arms were muscular as though he worked out. Shaking Harold's hand, Jake noticed a birth mark on his right arm that looked like the head of a horse. Harold's hair was cut short in a crew cut. Jake wondered if it was to conceal a receding hair line. Next to him, Cindy definitely looked like a trophy wife. Jake found himself wondered if Harold had money. They didn't look like a couple.

"Have you lived here long, Mrs. Rousseau?"

"Please, call me Cindy. We moved in next door about two months ago. Actually we're just renting from Mrs. Bowden," offered Cindy. "It was kind of your wife to invite us in."

"Mrs. Bowden?"

"You remember, Jake, the nice widowed lady who was living there when we were looking to buy this house."

"Sorry, I only vaguely remember seeing someone there. The whole house buying thing left me in something of a fog."

"Jake is better at remembering things a hundred years old or more. He used to be a history professor."

"Wow, that's impressive!"gushed Cindy. "Have you written any books?"

"A couple and some journal articles, mostly on the Civil War."

"War is hardly civil, is it Dr. Lowen?" volunteered Harold.

"War is hell, as the famous quotation goes. But please call me Jake."

"We don't want to overstay our welcome, do we, Cindy?"

"No. Thanks so much. You have been very kind. I hope we can see you again soon."

After their guests had left, Samantha observed. "What a strange couple. He seems so much older and less friendly. What does she see in him, anyway? I don't remember Mrs. Bowden saying anything about wanting to rent her place, do you? We may have been tempted to rent first before buying."

"I really don't remember the neighbor. I wouldn't have wanted to rent and move my books twice. I'm getting too old for that. And as far as what she sees in him, it's probably what's in his wallet and green that's his attraction. But you have not heard my news. Jasmine is a hero. She discovered a dead body."

Quickly filling Sam in on their adventure, Jake chided Sam for not coming along and missing all the fun.

"I wonder who the woman was?"

"There appeared to be no identification on or near the body. The police will see if her physical description matches any missing person reports. If not, then they'll have to rely on fingerprints, assuming she has her prints on file."

"But what if she didn't have a criminal record? Anyway, I thought you said her left arm was nothing but bones."

"When they uncovered her body, the right hand was intact. People have prints on file for lots of reasons. The FBI has over 30 million non-criminal fingerprint records, mostly of military, government, or authorized non-government personnel. So if the deceased had a criminal record or had an occasion to get into the FBI files, the cops will be able to make a positive ID."

"How long did the police think she was dead?"

11

"They can't be sure without running some tests and even then it might be iffy, but no more than two or three months, maybe less."

"So she might have been killed while we were out here looking for a house?"

"Or shortly thereafter."

"What did you say she looked like again?"

"Blond, about your height or a little, taller. Nice figure, but as I said, her face had been disfigured. I would guess that she could've been anywhere from 30 to 50 years old."

"About Mrs. Bowden's age?"

"I don't really remember seeing her so I can't say. Sam, are your detecting antenna up again?"

"Well, I have noticed our neighbors since we moved in but haven't been able to catch them outside to say hello till today. I guess I could have taken over a cake. Maybe I am old fashioned but I always thought that the neighbors brought stuff over to the newcomers. But it seems the Rousseaus are as new as we are."

"So?"

"So, Mrs. Bowden, who you have conveniently forgotten, probably because she was not a Civil War heroine, distinctly told me how much she loved the neighborhood and how she hoped to live here a long time. She made a point of explaining how settled she was and how great this place was to live. We made plans to get together when we moved here. Then when we got here she was gone."

"You're not suggesting the body Jasmine found is Mrs. Bowden?"

"I don't know. Stranger things than that have happened. Did the deputy give you a number to call?"

"Yes, but I told him I did not recognize the body."

"Well, I might give him a call."

Chapter Three

"Jake, there's a sheriff's deputy at the door to speak to you."

"Mr. Lowen, just have a couple more questions about the body you discovered yesterday."

"Certainly, be glad to help."

"Tell me again when you walked the Levee Trail last. Before yesterday, that is."

"We moved here about six weeks ago and I'm exploring the area. I walked there twice before, though I can't tell you exactly when. This is the first time I took the dog on that trail."

"Do you remember noticing anything before?"

"Honestly no. I'm just getting exercise, not looking for Indian artifacts or anything like that. But as I said, I usually take my camera with me, I'm a keen photographer."

"These some of your photos on the wall?"

"Yes, they are."

"They're really good, are you a professional?"

"More of an advanced amateur. I took a lot photos when I was working as a college history professor to illustrate my lectures."

"Western lore?"

"Civil War actually. I've toured all the major battle fields in the eastern part of the country."

"You mentioned that you might have some photos from the site that you found the body?"

"I'm sorry, I forgot to look. Absent minded professor is my excuse. How do you think that photos might help?"

"The medical examiner thinks the person was killed somewhere else and moved there. Also, he thinks the body was dead for some time before it was moved to the grave site."

"Give me a couple minutes to look on my computer for the digital images; I have them pretty well filed. Meanwhile can my wife get you a cup of coffee?"

"Thanks."

About twenty minutes later, Jake returned with a CD.

"Here are the images of the area. Hope it will be useful."

"I'm sure they will be. Your wife is a most charming hostess. She expressed an interest in seeing the body in case you two could identify the deceased."

"We would be glad to help, but we don't know many people here."

"Mrs. Lowen mentioned something about a neighbor who disappeared between the time you bought your home and when you moved in."

"She remembers her better than I do. I only saw her once."

"Still, any clue to her identity would be a help. We really don't have much to go on. The body doesn't match any missing person reports. If you like, you can ride with me and I can bring you back home or you can follow me in your car."

"If you don't mind, we'll follow you and run some errands on the way back.

Strapped in their Jeep, Samantha turned to Jake. "Gee, I was looking forward to a ride in a police car. Maybe I could have convinced him to turn on the lights and siren."

"Get serious, Sam. I don't know what we can add to this. Are you just sticking your nose into trouble again?"

"Jake, how can you say that?" Samantha smiled.

"Easy, I have known you for thirty-seven years and we've been married for thirty-five. I know when you're up to something and forming a theory. You're just a frustrated would be detective who reads too many mysteries."

"Jacob Lowen, first of all, you read nearly as many as I do. And second, you know I've honed my skills of observation over years of raising your children, teaching elementary school and watching your colleagues. Plus you write historical novels that usually have some detecting work or crime in them." Their retirement was largely funded by Jake's successful novels of which Samantha was an ardent fan and superb critic.

"Okay, Dr. Watson, what do you think?"

"I'm suspicious of that couple next door. Something didn't look right when they were over."

"Nothing wrong with Cindy Rousseau's looks. She is a stunning woman. Ouch! Don't hit me when I am driving."

"You keep thinking thoughts like that and when we get home, I will do more than punch your arm. And don't think I won't."

"Hey, why do you think I keep the guns and ammo locked up? You could be dangerous. I am sorry that I ever taught you to shoot."

"What I am thinking about my sharp kitchen knife would be better."

"Ouch again. Don't joke about that."

"Who's joking?"

"I was just agreeing with you that Cindy was not the type of wife one would normally associate with Harold, unless Harold had a lot of money."

"Jake, it's not just that Cindy and Harold don't look like a couple, though I agree with you there. But there was something in their manner, particularly his manner that didn't seem right. He couldn't wait to get out of our house. I never see him outside."

"Are you spying on the neighbors, Sam?"

"No, but in this pleasant weather, when I am sitting on the deck, I never see him out."

"Well, here we are. The deputy is motioning for me to park."

This was Sam's first experience in a morgue. Being naturally curious, she took in her surroundings.

"What a sterile place."

"What did you expect, Sam?"

"Probably not more, but there is something about being here that gives you a different sense from seeing it on TV. It really helps to be in an actual morgue."

"That is why I needed to travel to all those battlefields."

"The ones you dragged me and the kids to for every vacation?"

"They were learning experiences and we did catch a few beaches in all those trips. Anyway, it hasn't seemed to hurt them. They still like history."

15

When the attendant brought out the body, the deputy warned Sam and Jake that the body had suffered damage.

The Lowens studied the corpse.

"Have you seen this person before?"

"I'm sorry, officer, I cannot say for sure. There's a resemblance to Mrs. Bowden but the face has been so disfigured that I can't recognize this body. It could be her in size and hair coloring but that's not really enough to make a positive identification."

"That's okay, Mrs. Lowen, thanks for trying. We will follow up to see if anyone reported her missing. Do you know if the people renting her house have an address where they are sending the rental checks?"

"They said something about a six month rental. They said that Mrs. Bowden was given the opportunity to work in Thailand with an orphanage. They didn't have any more details."

"Well, we'll check it out. Thanks again for your help."

Driving back in the Jeep, Sam asked what the sheriff's office would do.

"Check her bank accounts, any church connections, probably interview the Rousseaus for more information."

"What a terrible thing to do, murder someone and then leave her body out there. Did the deputy say how she died?"

"Apparently strangled, then her face was bashed in, probably to avoid her being recognized."

"She apparently was wealthy or at least wore a lot of jewelry. You can still see the marks from her rings on her right hand."

"Why do you say that Sam?"

"Because most women wear one or perhaps two rings, usually on their left hands. If they wear a ring on their right hand, it would be on the ring finger. But some women wear a ring on each finger. That was what this lady did."

"Did Mrs. Bowden wear multiple rings?"

"On every finger of both hands, Jake. Most looked like family heirlooms."

"Well, whoever did it probably hoped the body wouldn't be found for years, if ever. Most serial killers taunt the police with the bodies of their victims in relatively easy to find places. So you can rest comfortably, Sam, there is probably not a serial killer on the loose in our area."

"With you to protect me, Jake, why would I be afraid?" as she reached out to touch his hand.

"Thanks for the vote of confidence. How about dinner out at that steakhouse we want to try? All this detecting work has given me a powerful appetite and anyway, I think I missed lunch."

"How you keep your trim figure with all you eat, Jake, is a wonder. But the steak house sounds good."

"Exercise, good genes and a high metabolism." Jake was a trim 181 pounds which was just right for his 6 foot two inch frame. No matter what he ate, he managed to stay the same, whereas Samantha was careful to watch her calories. It sometimes rankled her but she was quietly proud of the handsome man she was married to.

Returning home later that evening, the Lowen saw a sheriff's car outside their neighbors.

"Well, they didn't waste any time interviewing them. Wonder what they know about where Mrs. Bowden is?"

Chapter Four

Jake didn't give more thought to the mystery of the corpse, preferring instead to immerse himself in finishing his novel of a Union spy who encounters a former girlfriend during a reconnaissance of Atlanta in the advance Sherman's march. Jake was stuck on how to have his hero to extricate his romantic interest from harm's way while at the same time getting an important message through to Sherman. Jake's novels always seemed to have an alternative ending to history, if only this or that happened. Samantha called them his 'what if' novels but had to admit they were cleverly written with credible scenarios.

"Jake, mail's here."

"Anything special, anything from my publisher?"

"Just some bills … wait, there's a postcard. It's from Thailand."

"Who do we know in Thailand, one of our missionary friends?"

"Believe it or not, it is from our neighbor, Mrs. Bowden."

"No, really?"

"Really, says she is sorry that she wasn't here to greet us, but had a sudden opportunity to work in an orphanage and couldn't pass it up."

"What's the date?"

"You know how hard it is to read these postmarks. You take a look."

"This is dated a couple of days before I found the body."

"Well, it's not her."

"Maybe, but why would she send us a card?"

"Jake, I told you we connected."

"Sam, you are easy for people to like, but why now?"

"Coincidence?"

"Maybe? Did you notice the sheriff's car outside the neighbors the other day?"

"Yes, they weren't home the first time the deputy came by."

"Did they tell you what he does? I don't see them around."

"They didn't mention that, only something vague about property development. Apparently they moved here from Vegas."

"Did they tell you that?"

"No, it was something Cindy dropped casually in the conversation in passing. You know what I mean, Jake?"

"You mean something like, 'when I worked in Vegas?'"

"Yes, it sort of slipped out. Unless I'm mistaken, Harold gave her a 'look' and she dropped the subject."

"Sam, you may be right in suspecting our neighbors of hiding something, though it looks like they're clear of this murder. I'm going to call Deputy Lodestone. He is the one in charge of this case."

After a short phone call, Jake came back into their sunny kitchen with a view of the distant mountains.

"Well?"

"Apparently Mrs. Bowden is in Thailand. Lodestone checked with her bank and the lawyer handling her affairs while she is gone. The Rousseaus have a six month rental, furnished. Paid cash upfront; their choice not hers. Lawyer is the contact person if anything goes wrong. Backs up the story that it was a quick decision to go and fortunately, the Rousseaus turned up."

"Any indication they knew each other before?"

"None the deputy has turned up, but then he wasn't looking into that."

"Isn't he suspicious about the cash deal? Sounds like money laundering to me."

"They claim they just sold a house, had the cash and got a discount for paying up front. It's only three months more than first and last month plus a security deposit."

"Still, Jake, there's something funny going on, I can feel it in my bones."

"Speaking of bones, your bones feel lucky tonight? I'd like to visit the Casino Arizona at Salt River."

"Jake Lowen, in all my days! I never knew you were interested in casinos. You never visited the ones around Chicago, or were you sneaking out behind my back?"

19

"I haven't heard the expression in 'In all my days' since my Aunt Tillie died. That was her favorite expletive. Very conservative, Aunt Tillie. No I don't plan on gambling, but I have a feeling that we might see our elusive neighbors there."

"ESP?"

"P.U.G. Picking up garbage. I found a slip from Salt River on the street where it had blown out the neighbors can."

"Jacob Lowen! Are you snooping again?"

"Only being a historian, Sam. We are trained to look for clues. Most of history is sorting through the debris left behind and trying to piece together what happened."

"I never! …"

"That was Aunt Tillie's second favorite expression, Sam. Are you channeling Aunt Tillie?"

Ignoring Jake's comments, Samantha asked, "What time do you want to leave?"

"Let's catch supper there around seven, that's about when the neighbor's car pulls out of the driveway."

Chapter Five

"Well, that was a great meal, Jake. What's next on our agenda for this evening?"

"I thought a little turn around the various gaming areas might be interesting."

"And see who we might run into?"

"Actually, I would prefer not running into them or even being seen. Doesn't help if the other side knows you are conducting an intelligence mission. No, we are just here looking around. I still believe the best way to double your money is to fold it in half and stick it back into your pocket."

"Come on, Jake, don't you want to try our luck?"

"Sam, I will let you lose $10, no more."

"What's the best odds?"

"Well you could try the roulette wheel. The odds are 37 to 1 on a straight bet."

An hour later, Jake complimented Sam on her skill. "So you turned the $10 into $200, though you should have quit when you were up to $500."

"Let that be a lesson to me. Quit while you're ahead. In spite of winning I don't think I would get hooked on this."

"Good, let's ...."

Jake's conversation was interrupted by the sight of an angry and frustrated Harold Rousseau being dragged away from the craps table by Cindy.

"Come on, Harold, you've lost your limit for tonight."

"Damn it, Cindy. I need a bigger bankroll. After all, it's my money."

"I thought it was our money and at the rate you're losing it tonight it won't last long. Let's go."

"I want another drink."

"Harold, you're already drunk. No more."

"You bitch. You're just a gold digger. I should throw you back on the Vegas chorus line where I found you."

"Harold, this is not the time or place. Anyway, you need me more than I need you. Or have you forgotten?"

At that comment, Harold, though still belligerent, allowed himself to be dragged to the door.

"Did you see that show, Jake? I told you something wasn't right."

"What a scene. But did you hear how she subdued him?"

"That Harold's need of Cindy is more than physical?"

"Exactly, Sam. If it was really his money, and given their age difference it's probably true that he earned it. Maybe while married to his first wife and he's hiding assets on which wife number one has a claim. It's possible he's using Cindy to keep some assets that the court would give to his ex-wife otherwise."

"That would explain her comment that he needed her more because she could use the money without him being traced. But what about giving a social security number to the casino to report your winnings to the IRS?"

"That reminds me, Sam. Don't forget to report your winnings when we file our taxes. He could be using a fake social security number or just taking a chance and using his real number, figuring that they will be gone before the IRS catches up to them. Same with an ID, he could be using a fake driver's license or one issued in Cindy's last name."

"Is it that easy to obtain a fake ID?"

"If you know where to look, Sam. Thinking about leaving me and starting a new identity? If so, I get to keep the dog."

"Get serious you big lug! I was asking for purposes of playing detective. Though it would serve you right if I did leave you. Maybe then you would appreciate me."

"Darling Samantha, I do appreciate you and love you more than words can tell. Jasmine and I would be ever so lonely without you and anyway, how would I explain it to the children? Would I say their mother has run off to the circus?"

"Jacob Lowen, you would try the patience of a Job! Just answer my question."

"It's relatively easy to get a new identity, all the more so if you have a little political clout. One tried and proven way is to obtain a birth certificate of someone who was born about the same time you were but who died in childhood. Those can be obtained at an office of records. From there, you obtain a drivers license and a passport. The authorities are tightening down since 9/11 and getting a drivers license requires two forms of ID, but I think you could get a passport with just a certified copy of a birth certificate, hence the political clout to get a false birth certificate certified."

"I'm glad you are an honest man. You certainly know a lot of devious tricks."

"Part of being a historian. Aren't you glad you married me."

"Yes, but not because you know about criminal activity. What do you think is going on, Jake?"

"I think our neighbors are hiding from something or somebody. How about you?"

"I don't know Jake. But I'm thinking. Ready to go home?"

Chapter Six

For all his interests, Jake had the ability to shut out all distractions and focus in on one task for a long time. Sam always claimed he had ADD, but Jake would always counter even if he did, people with ADD were high achievers. Sam's comeback was just because someone earned a Ph.D. it did not mean that they didn't have other problems. To which Jake never had an answer, because it was all too true of many, if not the majority, of his colleagues.

Being in the zone, as he called it, meant that Jake worked solidly for the next week on his novel, finally feeling if it wasn't perfect, it was at least finished. Coming up for air, so to speak, he took Jasmine for a long walk around the neighborhood. He was just coming home when Cindy Rousseau pulled up in her driveway.

"Dr. Lowen, do you have a minute?"

"Sure, how can I help?" expecting to be asked to help carry in the bags of groceries he could see on the back seat.

"I need to talk to you. Could you come inside? Harold is out and I need to be able to talk to someone."

"We could go to my place, Samantha is out running errands, but she should be back soon."

"I'm expecting a phone call and need to be home, if you don't mind."

Once inside the kitchen and with the groceries removed from the car, Jasmine settled at Jake's feet while he waited for Cindy to begin.

"I know you and Mrs. Lowen saw us at the casino last week. I was so ashamed."

"It's okay. Those things happen. It looked like your husband had too much to drink and was not thinking straight."

"Actually, he's not my husband, not yet that is. He was married to a real bitch who made his life hell, no matter how well he provided for her. Finally he divorced her, but the settlement is dragging on and she is trying to bleed him for every cent he has. We are …, well, we are hiding out here from her until the court settlement is final. She just calls to berate him and belittle me or she would if she could find us."

"She doesn't know where you are?"

"No, Rousseau is my name, Harold's is …. Actually it would be better if you did not know."

"It's very tough to hide out these days, credit cards, driver's licenses, cell phones…."

"We know, we know," cutting Jake off. "That's why we pay cash when we can and why Harold isn't using his real name. It is also why we can't leave the country, at least not yet."

"Ergo, a six month rental?"

"That's right and everything that needs to be registered is registered or listed in my name. We don't think that anyone knows Harold is with me, at least we didn't. That's what I need to talk to you about. We think someone has recognized Harold."

"How? Where?"

"Harold gets so bored just sitting around the house with nothing to do. All he ever did was work and make money. His only relaxation was to gamble at casinos, mostly in Vegas. That is where we met. I was working at the Tropicana when I met Harold."

"How long ago was that?"

"About twelve months ago, maybe a little longer. He would come to town and we ….would see each other. He is really a nice guy, I grew fond of him and he told me about his wife and how terrible things were and how he was going to leave her."

"But things haven't quite worked out that way?"

"No, things have gotten ugly and well, I'm afraid for Harold."

"I can understand not wanting to have a confrontation, but…."

"Dr. Lowen, Harold's wife has connections to the mob. Her brother would kill Harold for dishonoring his little sister this way."

"So you two are laying low. Why tell me?"

"I had to tell somebody and I may need help with Harold. He is getting more and more morose and belligerent. You saw him the other night. I wonder if that type of behavior was what got the attention of the mob."

"Ms. Rousseau, I'm not a bodyguard. If you are really scared, you need police protection."

"But don't you see, if we go to the police, his wife will know. They are looking for him on a bench warrant. We can't involve the police."

Jake let out a low whistle. "Whew, you are in a tight bind! Maybe you should move on from here before your lease is up if you are that scared."

"But don't you see, they now know who I am. They can track us anywhere."

"No way of cutting a deal with them?"

"Dr. Lowen, do you know the difference between Harold's ex-wife and a terrorist? You can always negotiate with a terrorist."

"That bad. Well, I still don't see how I can help."

"Just keep your eyes open for strange cars and stranger men. Please let me know if you or Mrs. Lowen see anything."

"Do you want me to report anything suspicious to the police?"

"No, wait, maybe yes if they are doing anything that looks illegal. Maybe you can help us scare them off."

Jasmine let out a low growl. "Sounds like my wife's car, Jasmine knows the motor sound. I better be going. Can I tell Samantha what you told me?"

"Yes, and thanks for listening."

Later over coffee, Jake related the conversation to Sam.

"I wondered what you were doing coming out of their house, but then I saw you had a four-legged chaperon and I knew that you couldn't have gotten in any serious trouble."

"Thanks for your vote of confidence in my fidelity."

Samantha let out a soft laugh. "You're welcome. You know what would happen to you if you strayed. You should not have taught me to be such a good shot."

"I taught you for self defense."

"That will be my alibi when the cops come, 'Officer, I fired in self defense.'"

"Seriously, Sam, what do you make of her story?"

"It's plausible, but a little too convoluted for my taste. I think she is leaving out something and before your dirty mind goes there, I don't just mean about their relationship."

"Like what, Sam?"

26

"If this guy was so smart and so rich, he had to have a powerful lawyer or at least the sense to hire one. And if his wife was the spendthrift Cindy says she is, Harold would have been smart enough to salt some money away."

"He probably did and that is what he is living on now."

"And ex wants it?"

"Sounds reasonable. But actually I think you may be on to something. I had the feeling the whole time she was talking that it was a performance, staged just for my benefit."

"To what purpose, Jake?"

"That I don't know. Maybe she wants to leave him and is afraid of him. This gives her a 'witness' that there is something going on."

"So what are you going to do, Jake?"

"Nothing about this, but I will keep my eyes open just the same. What's for supper?"

Chapter Seven

"Leila called."

"Leila who?" asked Jake.

"Leila Espennelli."

"How's the weather in Chicago?"

"She didn't say, probably because she and Vinny are here in Phoenix."

Jake choked on his coffee and spluttered, "You didn't invite them over, did you?"

"How could I not? She's an old friend."

"And he's biggest blowhard I know. I can't abide being in the guy's company for more than five minutes. No, make that two minutes."

"Jake, what's so bad about Vinny?"

"What's so bad? What's so bad? Just that he is an insufferable braggart. Knows everybody and everything. Always trying to show how smart he is. If he doesn't know something, then he makes out as though it's not important."

"You're just mad because he thinks the Civil War is a useless subject."

"Sam, Vinny Espennelli thinks anything that doesn't revolve around his little world is a useless subject. The man has a brain the size of pea. If anything proved evolution, Vinny is exhibit "A." The guy is a genetic throwback to the Cro-Magnon period. I never could see what Leila sees in him. On the other hand, I could never figure out how you and she were friends. You have nothing in common."

"Jake, I have told you. Leila is an old school friend. She was awkward in school and the other girls picked on her. I defended her and that made her consider me a friend for life. I still feel sorry for her. She never seemed to get what was going on. I guess the word for it today would be spacey. Anyway they are in town looking at the possibility of retiring here and want to see us. I invited them to dinner tonight."

"What? Why did you do that? You know I can't stand the guy. He drives me nuts."

"It was either that or drive over to their hotel for dinner and worry about him sticking you with the check after he has ordered the most expensive wine on the menu. Not to mention the cocktails he consumes beforehand."

But here, in our home, it'll ruin the atmosphere for me. I'll need to light candles and hire Navajo *Hataɫii* to cleanse the house after he leaves."

Jacob Lowen, you are exaggerating again!"

"Okay, Sam. I won't need candles, just the *Hataɫii."* Jake was of course referring to the Navajo tradition of cleansing a dwelling from evil influences. He had been reading up on Navajo religion in preparation of his first western novel.

Jake sulked in his study the rest of day, put off from writing. Even a long walk in the McDowell Sonoran Preserve with Jasmine did little to lift his mood. Jasmine on the other hand while seemingly conscious of her master's mood still managed to enjoy the smells of their adventure

For Jake it was as though Paradise had been invaded and polluted by an evil presence. Vinny Espennelli was a shallow vain man who traded on the fact that his brother was a reputed mobster. Vinny himself was too dumb for even the mob to trust and had been set up in a dry cleaning business. The business was a front to launder money for the mob, a joke that wasn't lost on even Vinny. Once when Jake had been forced by Sam to visit the Espennelli home, Vinny was drunk and confided as much to Jake. Vinny didn't go into the store very much. It was run by some illegal immigrants who slaved over the cleaning end. One who had a decent command of English worked the front desk. Well, at least Vinny will be used to hearing Spanish if they move here, though Jake was fairly certain Vinny's command of Spanish ended with a couple of simple commands and some Spanish swear words and insults.

It would be terrible if they moved out here, but what could Jake do? An idea formed in his mind that would be risky and involve spending more time with the Espennellies but if it worked would insure they would not move to Arizona. His mood improved, he turned around and headed back to the parking area with Jasmine who was reluctant to give up her exploration of new smells.

Dinner was tolerable. For one thing, Vinny didn't drink since he was terrified of getting another DUI conviction. One more and the law would take his license away. He confided to Jake that he wasn't sure if Arizona and Illinois had a connection that way, but he just couldn't take the chance. Since he wasn't drinking, he wasn't nearly as belligerent as he usually got. And since Jake was retired, he apparently posed less of a threat to Vinny's fragile ego. So Vinny laid off trying to best Jake the way he had when Jake was still a professor. Jake, in his better moments felt sorry for Vinny. Too much good Italian cooking had left distinctly rotund and weighing something like a pro football defensive lineman. Unfortunately, Vinny was short for his weight, standing about Samantha's height in what Jake knew to be platform shoes. So he was probably 5'6" in his stocking feet. With his stomach spilling over his belt, he could have played a Christmas Santa Claus without any extra padding. Jake thought it was a good bet that part of Vinny's bravado was to compensate for his short stature.

Vinny complained about the heat and the way nothing was like it was back home. Jake was puzzled by this since all the same shops and restaurants were located in Phoenix until he realized that Vinny meant that he was not recognized by maitre d's and head waiters in the restaurants, which meant they expected him to pay for his meals instead of covering the check for fear of his brother. He kept comparing the treatment he received back home in Chicago to the lousy service here in Phoenix.

As Jake had expected, the dinner conversation after he had voiced his dissatisfaction of Phoenix was devoted to Vinny boasting of his mob connections and the news of what was happening in Chicago. Jake was listening with half an ear while thinking about the plot of another novel when something Vinny said brought him back into the conversation.

"So, like, this guy is in real trouble. He stole twenty million of the mob's money and left town. Even his wife didn't know where he went."

"Who are you talking about, Vinny? asked Jake.

"Aren't you paying attention, Jake, or have too many years of teaching dulled your brain? I was talking about Harry Gianelli, the guy who was bribing state officials so they would throw lucrative contracts to the mob without competitive bids. Hell, it cost the taxpayers three or four times what it should because of what he was doing. Makes me glad that I cheat on my taxes so I don't get ripped off."

Jake hoped he successfully suppressed from showing the shudder he felt inside and wondered again what it cost to have a *Hatalii* perform a cleaning ceremony. He also wondered if they had any candles he could light after their guests left as part of his own private cleansing ceremony. "So how did this Gianelli get the twenty million?"

"He was holding back on the bribes and also getting some kickback from the contractors. The FBI is conducting an investigation on corruption in Chicago City government and a contractor who Harry had squeezed for too much money coughed him up in a plea bargain. Harry got out just before the feds got to him. Also just ahead of the mob who have their own mole in the investigating team. Left his wife Carolyn high and dry. Cleaned out all their accounts, even stole his wife's jewelry. She was really pissed. Rumor has it she's working with the boys to track the scumbag down before the Feds find him."

"When was all this, Vinny?"

"About three months ago. Wife disappeared about a week or two later. I overheard my brother saying that she had a lead on Harry and had taken out after him."

"Vinny, you know Vittelo wouldn't like you talking about family business ..." protested Leila.

30

"Shut up, Leila. I'll tell you when I want you to speak. Anyway, Jake isn't anybody anymore. He won't talk, will'ya Jake?"

Jake and Sam shot each other looks of disgust at Vinny's treatment of Leila. "No, Vinny, I won't tell. What do Harry and Carolyn look like?"

"Harry's pretty nondescript. Looks like anybody else. Carolyn is a looker. She's still a classy broad. Blonde hair, tall, good build. Was a model before marrying Harry. Not my type though, I prefer a woman to be voluptuous, don't I, honey?"

Leila blushed at that remark."Yes, honey. You do." Leila was distinctly Rubenesque. Shorter than Vinny, Leila was a testimony to her good cooking. 'Never trust a thin cook' was the motto of Jake's Aunt Tillie and she had had the figure to testify to her culinary skills.

Trying to get back on the subject, Jake pursued the topic. "Did Carolyn try to follow her husband alone?"

"Naw, Willie the Cook was assigned to go with her."

"Willie the Cook?"

"That's what they call him because he always cooks his marks a meal, usually breakfast, before he kills them, Jake."

"They just sit there and watch him cook?"

"Usually they're tied up. Mostly he feeds them if he doesn't think it is wise to untie them. Calls it serving a condemned man his last meal. Victims are found with food spilled down their clothes because it is rumored he force feeds his victims."

"Rumored?"

"Willie works alone Jake. Prefers it that way. No witnesses, not even guys from his side. It would be hard to get a conviction if they did charge him. After all it is not against the law to like to cook." Vinny laughed at his own joke so hard that he started to choke.

This man is disgusting thought Jake and a glance at Sam made him understand that she felt the same way.

Later cleaning up after their guests left, Jake asked Sam what she was thinking.

"The same thing you are. I'm wondering if our mystery body is none other than Carolyn Gianelli."

Jake wondered if he really needed to go through with the plan he had hatched on his walk, but it was too late to back out. Samantha had already mentioned it to Leila and she was overjoyed to spend time with her best friend Samantha. But Jake was pretty sure it would kill any idea of the Espennellies coming to live in Arizona. To ensure that outcome was worth a day of his time.

The next day went off better than Jake had hoped. Vinny had not changed overnight. In fact, he was as obnoxious as ever. More questioning about Gianelli did not yield any more information, just repeated assertions by Vinny that Gianelli was in deep doo doo and that when the mob got him it would be curtains. Asked if Vinny thought Carolyn had been in on his disappearance and had merely waited to join him, Vinny explained to Jake, in language reminiscent of that he used to speak to someone Vinny regarded as retarded, that was the point of Willie the Cook going with Carolyn. Both Harry and Carolyn might have been fed breakfast by Willie the Cook.

Jake's plan involved exploiting one of Vinny's weaknesses, actually a couple of them. Vinny was deathly afraid of heights and had a tendency to get car sick. Meeting them at their hotel, Jake and Sam joined the Espennellies in their rental car, a large Lincoln Towncar. Vinny took the wheel for the trip up to Sedona, then yielded it to Jake for the ride through Oak Creek Canyon. The beautiful vistas and hairpin turns were lost on Vinny who held on to the grab bar above the door in terror as Jake skillfully negotiated the winding road. It was about a third of the way through the canyon as they were descending a left hand hairpin turn that Vinny threw up for the first time. He hadn't been able to get his window open and covered himself and the dashboard. Stopping to let him clean up, Vinny swore that he would never live in such a god-forsaken place. Forced by the women to slow down, Jake navigated the remainder of the canyon at such a moderate pace that he was constantly being passed by other drivers. Even that did not help Vinny as he hung his head out of the window and threw up twice more.

The drive from Flagstaff to the Grand Canyon was a somber affair. The group had considered turning back to Phoenix but Leila pleaded they go on since she realized she would never get Vinny back here again. Vinny was too sick to say anything and after a quick stop at the canyon's edge to take photos of Leila peering into the abyss, they headed home. Vinny had missed seeing the canyon, having instead lain across the backseat moaning.

Back home in Scottsdale, Sam turned to Jake. "That was a mean thing to do, Jacob Lowen!"

"Whatever do you mean, Samantha?"

"You remembered that Vinny hates heights and can get desperately carsick. You took him on that road on purpose."

'Maybe I did and maybe I didn't. But think of it this way. If they had moved out and he hated it, think how miserable they would be. He might have even fallen off the edge of the Grand Canyon."

"Jake, you were only thinking about how miserable you would be if they moved out here. On the other hand, I might forgive you if you really acted for their best interests."

"Scout's honor. What's for dinner?"

Chapter Eight

"Who was that on the phone, Sam?"

"Leila Espennelli. She wanted to thank us for the taking the time to drive them to the Grand Canyon. She said Vinny wouldn't have taken her but he had to go because we asked them."

"How is Vinny, anyway?"

"Apparently totally recovered and off gambling at a casino."

"Wonder if he is going to Talking Stick?"

"Leila wasn't interested in going so she didn't pay attention. Why do you care?"

"Because, Sam, when I was walking Jasmine, I saw Harold leave the house without Cindy. I was wondering if he was headed there himself."

"So?"

"So, Sam, I'm curious if either Vinny recognizes Harold or Harold recognizes Vinny."

"Do you think Harold is Harry Gianelli?"

"Maybe, that's one thought. But I am wondering if Harold has connections in Chicago."

"Jake, there is a better chance that Harold is Harry."

"What kind of odds are you offering on that bet, Sam?"

"I am smarter than to bet against you, professor. What are you going to do?"

"I'm feeling lucky, want to go the casino again?"

"What's my limit to lose this time, Jake?"

"In spite of your winnings last time, it is still $10."

"What happened to my $200?"

"Technically, you only won $190, but it went to the western dress you bought to join me in the Cowboy Shooting events."

"Oh! Okay, only this time when I get a pile I am going to quit."

'That's what all gamblers say, Sam."

Sam's luck did not match her first time outing and she quickly lost her money. They'd decided to have dinner at the casino and before entering the dining room wandered around the various gaming areas.

"Are you cured, Sam?"

"What do you mean?"

"I mean from gambling. I would hate to see even losing $10 become a habit or worse an addiction."

"Yes, I am. It is fun to win. But there aren't many winners are there?"

"The odds always favor the house, Sam. That's how they stay in business."

"Jake, those people playing slots look like zombies."

"It's just the light, honey, they are real people."

"No, I don't mean that, I mean that they are just staring at the machines like they were mindless creatures."

"Some of them are. You are looking at people addicted to the slots and are feeding the machines mechanically."

Suddenly Sam touched Jake's arm. "Isn't that Vinny?"

"Yeah, he is playing blackjack."

"Well at the craps table by the door, Harold Rousseau, if that is his real name, is throwing the dice and a crowd is gathering around."

"He must have some hot dice."

"Hot dice?"

"Slang for doing really well at craps. When someone is on a roll it always attracts a crowd."

"Look, Jake. Vinny has left his table and is drifting over."

"He's very interested in the shooter."

"Shooter, oh, the guy with the dice, Harold?"

"Yeah. Look at the expression on Vinny's face, Sam. It's like he found something."

"Here he comes, Jake."

"Hi Vinny. Feeling better?"

"Oh, yeah, Jake, sure. Feeling great. 'Scuse me, I gotta run."

"That was the shortest conversation I ever had with Vinny in my life, Sam."

"Jake, not only was he in a hurry. He seemed frightened."

"You're right. Who do you think he recognized?"

"Someone he seemed afraid of. Whatever, he was in a real hurry to get out of here."

"Look over at the table, the crowd is drifting away."

"Maybe Harold is quitting while he is ahead for a change."

"What if he lost his whole pile of chips, Jake?"

"Not much chance of that, he is smiling and anyway he is carrying a pile of chips to cash them in."

"He's heading this way, should we move so he doesn't see us?"

"Nah, we're not following him if he passes by we can say hello if he notices us."

But Harold didn't notice them. He was too flush in the glow of his winnings to notice anyone. After he cashed out, Jake got an inspiration. Walking up to the window, he asked the cashier if the man who just cashed out was Harold Rousseau.

"I'm sorry sir. We don't divulge the names of our patrons."

"Hey, that's okay. This guy Harold Rousseau and I were in high school together and I haven't seen him in years. If that's not Harold, it's somebody who looks a lot like him. But I don't want to make a fool out myself going up to a stranger. Can you just tell me if it's not Harold Rousseau?"

"Well, I've had the same experience thinking it was someone else. I still can't give you his name, but Harold Rousseau was not the name he used when I issued him his W-2G."

Rejoining Samantha, Jake recounted his exchange with the cashier.

"So, he's using an assumed name?"

"Sam, for all I know he used his real name. We know Rousseau is a fake name."

"But you talked about how easy it was to get a fake identity."

"It is, but we don't know if the name our neighbor used is his real name. For all we know, whatever name he gambles under is also false."

"Why do you think that Vinny left in such a hurry?" asked Sam.

"I don't know, but that blowhard was scared or excited or both."

"Jake, could Harold be 'Willie the Cook?'"

"You might be on to something, Sam. Let's discuss it over dinner. I'm starved."

Chapter Nine

Coming in from taking Jasmine on her morning run, Jake found Sam just getting off the phone with a puzzled look on her face.

"Who's that?"

"That was Leila. She and I were to have a facial at the Aji Spa in Chandler and then catch lunch."

"Great, when are you going?"

"We're not. Vinny got back from the casino last night and told her they were leaving as soon as possible. They're catching a plane this morning."

"Some problem?"

"Leila's not sure; Vinny doesn't tell her much about his work. But he seemed troubled to her last night. She wanted to try a Chinese restaurant someone recommended to her, but Vinny insisted on getting room service. When the tray came, he made her open the door while he hid in the bathroom."

"Doesn't sound like our boy?"

"No, it doesn't Jake. He sounds scared to me."

"Me too. Do you think it was someone he saw at the casino, Sam?"

"I think so. It fits in. The question is who? Harold or someone else? A lot of people crowded around that table."

"Bet you dollars to donuts it was Harold or the man we know as Harold, whatever his name really is."

"Do you think he would open up to you if you asked him Jake?"

"Not if he's that scared. Remember, as dimwitted as I think he is, his brother is a big time mobster and Vinny has seen him in operation. No, something put our boy off."

"You're probably right. Gee, I was really looking forward to the spa treatment; we were going to get the Kahagam."

"Kahagam, it sounds like a disease, Sam."

"It's their signature facial treatment, the Bluebird facial. The spa uses ancient Navajo treatments."

'They put a bird on your face? Doesn't sound that great to me."

'For someone with so much education, you aren't so smart, Jake. The Bluebird is a luxurious Jasmine scented treatment tones and rejuvenates the skin. They use two separate masks on your face. The brochure says "The entire experience will leave your skin looking and feeling tighter, toned, and hydrated."

"Masks, huh. Sounds like something out of the Lone Ranger. 'Return with us now to those exciting days of yesteryear ....'"

"I don't know why I put up with you, Jacob Lowen."

"Look, if it means that much to you, I will drive down with you and after your facial we can still have lunch there."

"And what will you do while I'm having my seventy minute facial?"

"Well, there's a used book store in Chandler I wanted to check out...."

"Can you be cleaned up and ready to leave in an hour?"

"Yep, but I think I want to call Deputy Sheriff Lodestone first."

"Going to tell him about Harry Gianelli?"

"Yes and about Vinny's strange reaction yesterday."

"So Harold is Willie the Cook laying low for a while with Harry Gianelli's money?"

"Could be. My biggest problem is how to explain this to Lodestone without having him think I'm in the mob myself. You've got to admit it's a fairly complex story."

"I'm sure you're up to it, Jake."

Actually the conversation with Lodestone went better than he could have expected. The deputy didn't seem troubled by his connection with Vinny Espennelli and accepted Jake's explanation that his wife and Vinny's wife were school friends. Lodestone confirmed they had not identified the woman Jasmine had found and promised to follow up the lead on Carolyn Gianelli if for no other reason than to eliminate another possibility.

Over lunch, Jake had to admit that Sam's face did look more toned and hydrated which what she wanted to hear. It also made it possible for Sam to overlook the books Jake had stashed in the back of the Jeep after his successful trip to the bookstore.

When they got home, there was a message on their answering machine from the Maricopa Medical Center asking Mrs. Samantha Lowen to please call back.

"I didn't know you were sick, Sam?"

"I'm not and I have never been there. I wonder what's up?"

Calling the number Sam was transferred to the ER.

"I'm Mrs. Samantha Lowen; can I ask why you called?"

"Mrs. Lowen, a friend of yours, Leila Espennelli was admitted in serious condition. Before taking her into surgery, she asked for you. Our desk clerk located your number through directory assistance."

"Leila! What happened to her? Is she okay?"

"She is still in surgery. She was shot at her hotel."

"Shot! By who? Can I see her?"

"If you come over, you can wait for the doctor to come out when he's done with the operation."

"I'll be right over."

On the way to the Medical Center, the couple puzzled over the strange news.

"Why didn't Vinny call, Jake?"

"I don't know Sam. He was acting strange when he left the casino, like he had seen a ghost."

"Yes, but whose ghost, Jake? I wonder if he called anyone in Chicago?"

"Leila didn't mention it to you this morning, did she?"

"No, but he could have called from the lobby or his cell phone."

"I wonder what happened to Vinny."

The answer to that question was supplied by the news on KNFX reporting on a murder at the Holiday Inn.

"While details are still pending, we can report that a man had been killed and a woman, apparently his wife, is in serious condition at Maricopa Medical Center. The dead man had been not yet officially been identified, but News Radio KNFX has learned from sources at the hotel that the couple were found in a room registered to Vinny Espennelli, a Chicago resident who was vacationing with his wife. Both were apparently shot multiple times. Police speculate that robbery might have been the motive as the victims' wallets were missing. More details as they become available. Back to studio ….."

Jake lowered the volume on the radio. "Whoa! I take back all the nasty things I thought about Vinny. Even he didn't deserve to die in Phoenix."

"I wonder if Leila will make it?" said Sam with real sorrow in her voice.

"If what we're thinking is right, there should be a police guard on Leila. Dial 911 on the cell phone and see if we can get a message to Deputy Lodestone."

The 911 operator kept asking Sam the nature of the emergency and where should help be dispatched. Finally in exasperation, Sam asked for and got the non-emergency number of the Sheriff's office.

After some delay, Deputy Sheriff Lodestone came on the line. Quickly Sam explained Leila's call this morning canceling their meeting. She also repeated the observed nervousness of Vinny at the casino. Sam suggested that consideration be given to a police guard over Leila since apparently she could identify her attacker.

Reaching the hospital, Jake and Sam rushed to the waiting room outside the OR. After an hour wait, a doctor in green scrubs came out to talk with them.

"Mrs. Lowen?"

"Yes!"

"I'm Dr. Ramawhaldi. I performed the surgery on Mrs. Espennelli."

"How is she? Is she going to make it?"

"It's too early to tell. The next twenty four hours are critical. She lost a lot of blood and there was a lot of internal damage. Fortunately, the bullets missed her heart, but not by much. One lung is deflated. It's amazing she survived at all. The man with her was not as lucky; he died in the hotel room."

"Can I see her?"

"I'm afraid not. She's unconscious and in very serious condition. We are monitoring her vital signs."

Speaking for the first time, Jake asked: "Is there a police guard on duty?"

41

"A police guard? Whatever for?" puzzled Dr. Ramawhaldi.

"Because this was no ordinary robbery. This may have been a mob related killing. Mrs. Espennelli is in danger. Those responsible may try to finish the job."

Dr. Ramawhaldi was thoughtful. "To be honest, Mrs. Espennelli may not pull through in any case."

"Can I stay with her?" asked Sam.

"You can't be in the room, but I will arrange for you to be outside her door in ICU when she comes out of recovery."

"Sam, you go down to the Emergency Room and find out how they knew to call you. I'll take the first watch outside her room until we get some cops up here," volunteered Jake.

Splitting up, Jake kept watch over Leila's room, trying to note who looked like they belonged in the ICU.

Samantha had some trouble locating the nurse who initially treated Leila as the ER was crowded with patients. After some time, she was able to speak to Sandy Black.

"I'm not sure I can tell you much, Mrs. Lowen. She was pretty weak from shock and loss of blood."

"Surely she told you something that made you call me?"

"Well, all she kept whispering between gasping for breath was 'Samantha Lowen, Scottsdale, call her.'"

"That's all?"

"Yes. We were so busy trying to save her life I didn't have a chance to try to call you until 90 minutes later."

"Thanks for calling."

"I had to Mrs. Lowen, Mrs. Espennelli fixed her eyes on me and I can't forget the pleading that was in her eyes."

"How did you find us? We only moved in a couple of months ago. We aren't in the directory."

"The old fashioned way, I called directory assistance." Sandy Black said with a soft laugh.

'Tell me honestly, do you think she'll make it?"

"Mrs. Lowen, she is very badly hurt, but they have a first class trauma unit here. If she makes it any place, it would be here. But if you're a praying person, it wouldn't hurt to pray for her. I am."

Meeting Jake outside ICU, Sam quickly shared what she had learned.

"Vinny recognized somebody last night at the casino, but who?"

"It couldn't have been Harold Rousseau or whatever his real name is, because his back was to Vinny, Sam."

"Jake, you know that you can often recognize a person from behind, by the way they walk or the shape of their head. What if he recognized Harold Rousseau that way?"

"Okay, I'll grant you that. But Harold never turned around. He was too busy rolling dice. It has to be someone else. Someone that Vinny was frightened of. Look at the way he didn't want to leave his room. Didn't Leila say that he ordered in room service last night?"

"Jake, I love you, you're a genius!"

"Thanks, I love you too and thanks for recognizing my talents, but …."

"Don't you see? Room service. The Espennellis ordered supper and breakfast this morning from room service."

"Sam, are you thinking that Vinny recognized Willie the Cook?"

"Exactly. We are assuming that he was interested in Harold Rousseau, but what if it wasn't Harold but Willie he saw?"

"Didn't Vinny say that Willie had accompanied Carolyn Gianelli to look for her husband? And that Willie had not reported back to Chicago?"

"I think so, Jake. What if Willie and Carolyn found Harry Gianelli and killed him for the money?"

"But where is Carolyn? Is that her body Jasmine found?"

"Where is Willie, Jake? Do we even know what he looks like?"

"We need to call in the professionals, Sam."

Chapter Ten

Jake and Sam stayed on duty until Deputy Lodestone arrived with another officer. Sam explained what they thought and stressed that Leila might still be in danger from her assailant. Lodestone described the crime scene.

"Looks like she opened the door to the guy. Had a breakfast tray like he was room service, but it was just a tray that had been left outside another room after an early breakfast. Mr. Espennelli was shot in the doorway of the bedroom. He seemed to be the target; the guy emptied five shots into him, three in the chest, two in the head. He was dead before he hit the floor. Must have grabbed the missus and used her as a shield or just to keep her from running. She was shot at close range in the back, twice. There was a grazing wound on the side of her head, looked like he was going for a head shot but missed. Probably emptied his gun, we found eight .45 hulls on the floor. Also probably wanted out of there before anyone came to see what the noise was."

"Did the shooter use a silencer?" Jake was always curious about weaponry.

"No, that is what is strange if it was a professional hit. But a .45 can malfunction with a silencer and this guy wanted to be sure, ergo the number of slugs pumped into Mr. Espennelli. The room on one side was empty but the other side heard the sound and called the desk."

"Did anyone investigate?" asked Sam.

"The neighbors couldn't identify the direction of the sound, thought it might be next door. Desk called Espennelli's room, didn't get a response. Before they could send someone to check, the real room service guy showed up and knocked. When there was no answer, he used a house phone to call the desk. The desk clerk sent someone up and they discovered the bodies."

"We saw Vinny at the casino last night and he seemed agitated. Jake and I think he recognized somebody he was afraid of."

"Any idea who that might be?" inquired Lodestone.

"No, most of the people had their backs to us and therefore to Vinny. But he beat it out of there and hunkered down until …." volunteered Sam.

"Do you have contact numbers for them in Chicago, Mrs. Lowen?"

"Probably at home, yes, I'm sure I can find out who to contact. Where can I call you?"

Driving home in the early evening light, the Lowen discussed the day and how to communicate with Leila's relatives.

'I wish you had let me stay, Jake."

'Honey, there's nothing you can do. The nurses won't let you stay in her room and promised to call you if Leila's condition changes."

"Still …."

"Still you have pity on her as the awkward schoolgirl you befriended. I am more worried about her brother in law. He is bound to come to town to avenge his brother's murder, no matter what a dipstick he knew him to be."

"You mean, I can criticize my family, but don't you dare, right, Jake?"

"Yeah, that's the code that we Eastern Mediterranean's live by."

"We Eastern Mediterraneans?"

"Well, Sam, you know that I'm part Jewish."

"On your grandfather's side."

"Hey, Sam, that's who I am named for: Jacob Lowenstein. He married Efigenia Katsandoulos who was Greek, but you know all this!"

"I just enjoy getting a rise out of you when you pull that Eastern Mediterranean stuff."

Sam quickly found the number of Leila's parents who, though in their eighties, seemed alert. Giving them the best possible report on Leila's condition and promising to keep them informed, Sam obtained from them Vinny's brother's phone number.

"How did they take it, Sam?"

"As expected. They asked about coming out to be with her. I promised to let them know. If they come out, I offered to let them stay with us. Would you call Vitello?"

Vitello Espennelli had already been contacted by the authorities in Phoenix. However, he was interested in what the Lowens could relate about the night in the casino. Vitello had booked a flight and wanted to see Jake and Samantha after he had viewed his brother's body for a positive ID and looked in on his sister-in-law. Vitello mentioned that he would be accompanied by some of his associates who would be staying on to look into matters from the viewpoint of the family.

"How did Vitello seem?"

"Well, Sam, as I explained before, we Mediterraneans consider family all important. Whatever sins or shortcomings Vinny had are forgotten. The family honor must to upheld and Vinny and Leila be avenged."

"Jake, I wish we could figure out who Vinny saw that caused him to flee in terror. Did his brother say if Vinny had called?"

"Actually, Vinny did call Vitello, but Vitello was involved in a business meeting and couldn't be interrupted. Vinny refused to leave a message, only that he would be cutting short his trip and would see him as soon as he got home."

"A business meeting that took all night? Oh, that kind of business."

"Vitello didn't actually say that. It's only a supposition, though probably a correct one, Sam."

"So whatever Vinny saw, he only felt safe relaying directly to Vitello."

"Right, so Vitello may have a clue to this mystery. Whether he will share it with the police or take care of it in his own way is the $64,000 Question."

"Jake, that's such an old allusion, it really dates you."

"It also dates you if you get it."

Several times that evening, Sam called the hospital for Leila's condition. She remained in stable but critical condition. Finally, Jake convinced her that they both needed to get some rest as tomorrow promised to be a busy day. Just after they dropped off to sleep, Jake was awakened by the sound of a noisy argument coming from the Rousseaus' house. Going to the window, he saw the Harold pulling Cindy into the house, as she resisted. While Jake couldn't make out what they were saying, catching only the occasional word, it was obvious they were both angry. One of the phrases he did catch was "you've gone too far."

Too awake to sleep, having had the edge taken off his fatigue, Jake went to the computer. Initially intending to work on his novel, Jake found himself instead searching the net for news items on Harry Gianelli. What he found was pretty much what Vinny had told him, but there were details Vinny left out, such as the specifics of Gianelli's alleged connections with Chicago political figures. Gianelli was an intimate friend of the mayor and a frequent visitor to his mansion. Mrs. Carolyn Gianelli was a fashion plate and seen in all the right places. Carolyn had been a model and was a striking beauty. What Jake found strange was that there were few photos of Harry and none close enough to see his face clearly. All were snapshots taken at various events. The photos did show a powerfully built and trim man, who looked physically fit. Harry, at least from what Jake could determine, was camera shy. In spite of his glamorous wife, he seemed to prefer to work behind the scenes. It certainly fit with a mob figure, but it also could be the persona of a political fixer.

On a whim, Jake also googled Cindy Rousseau. It was pretty much as he expected. She had a web site and there were one or comments posted by ardent fans. The publicity photos were striking. It would be easy to see how Harold would be attracted to her. If he were married to a woman his own age, it would be hard for his wife to compete. If Harold's ex-wife was the harpy that Cindy portrayed her as, all the more so. The argument that had woken him up, however, reinforced the notion that all was not well between Harold and Cindy. Jake thought back to the conversation with Cindy in the Rousseaus' kitchen. At the time he wondered if it had been staged for his benefit by Cindy. Now he wasn't as sure. Was she really afraid of Harold? Did she have reason to be afraid? Jake reflected he really didn't know much about Harold. He didn't even know his real name, let alone what he did for a living.

Jake was tempted to take Jasmine for a late night walk. The moon was full causing the landscape to have a luminosity that beckoned him. Trying not to wake about Sam, Jake gathered up his clothes and dressed in the guest bathroom. He snatched up his Taurus revolver, the Judge, which he normally loaded with a combination of .410 shells and .45 Colt solids. Usually for walking in snake country the first three rounds up were .410 shot, followed by two .45 solids. Jake figured the same configuration would serve him well for a waltz around the neighborhood. Not that he was expecting trouble, but there had been reports of a rabid raccoon in the greater Phoenix area and Jake didn't like to take unnecessary chances.

Jake tried to convince himself it was because he couldn't get to sleep. But as he found himself planning his walk to include two passes of the Rousseaus' house, he knew he wanted to satisfy his curiosity if there were still lights burning. His perambulation, during which Jasmine savored the night smells up close and personal, did not yield any solutions to his mystery. He did take the opportunity to examine the plate on the car parked the driveway. He remembered Cindy opening the garage with a remote and was vaguely aware when he had helped with the groceries that both bays had cars in them. It had not struck Jake as strange at the time, but the more he thought about it now, the more puzzled he was. It was a two car garage, yet most of the time both Harold's and Cindy's cars were in the driveway. Presumably Mrs. Bowden had left her automobile parked in the garage, but he doubted the widow would have had two cars. Yet, now there was only one car parked in the driveway. Jake wondered if he could somehow get in and examine the plates on the cars in the garage.

Unmolested by raccoons, rabid or not, Jake and Jasmine returned home and after fixing himself a warm glass of milk, Jake fell asleep. In the morning, he remembered he had dreamt about a mutilated corpse, very much like the one Jasmine uncovered and had the strong sense the victim was trying to tell him something.

Chapter Eleven

Over breakfast, Jake admitted to Sam his confusion over the number of cars parked next door at the Rousseaus'.

"Do you remember if Mrs. Bowden had two cars in her garage, Sam?"

"Normally, I wouldn't notice cars. That is your thing, but I do remember her mentioning she had an empty bay since she only had one car but a two car garage. Why do you ask?"

"Remember when I helped Cindy in with her groceries and she confided in me?"

"That you would have gone into her house still bothers me, but yes."

"Hey, I had Jasmine as my bodyguard. She wouldn't have let me cheat on you with Cindy."

"That dog is devoted to you. I'm going to reserve judgment on whether she is a credible character witness. What's your point in bringing this up? Are you ready to confess something?"

"No, I'm not confessing anything because there is nothing to confess except stupidity."

Samantha interrupted Jake, "You got that right, lover."

"Look, will you just listen and stop playing the jealous wife. You know that I am a one woman man…"

"And you better stay that way!"

"Sam, I am trying to tell you something important. Please. When I was there, there were two cars parked in the garage. Cindy's car was in the driveway."

"So?"

"So, one was Mrs. Bowden's. Whose was the other car?"

"Harold's?"

"Couldn't be, Harold was out. Cindy said so when we were talking. Anyway, I noticed when he came home a few minutes later in another car."

"Maybe he's a car collector, like you."

Jake winced at the slam from his wife about Jake's propensity to have a bunch of automobiles at any given time. He had sold his collection before moving out to Arizona for two reasons. One he didn't want to move them and more importantly he could acquire new, rust free vehicles in Arizona, including a convertible or two. "No, not like me. Both the cars in the garage were nondescript sedans, not even a coupe let alone a ragtop."

"Maybe he just likes sedans?"

"Harold isn't the collector type. I can tell."

"You haven't seen enough of him to know what type he is, Jake?"

"True, but a real car buff takes his cars out and at least washes them."

"Okay, so he's not a real car buff, I still don't see your point."

"If we could get the plate numbers on their cars, we could have Lodestone run a check on who they're registered to."

"And how do you propose to do that?"

"A little reconnaissance, Sam. A little reconnaissance."

Thinking it would be several days before both of the Rousseau cars were gone from the driveway and Jake had the opportunity to look into the garage, he was surprised when later in the afternoon he noticed that both cars were gone. Taking the opportunity to look in from the side door which was half glass, Jake noted that there was only one car in the garage. From the angle he was looking in from, he had difficulty making out the plate number, but got enough of it to guess at what the first letter was which he could just make out.

Worried that Lodestone would think he was on a wild goose chase, he never the less called the deputy and asked him see if Rita Bowden's plate started with that letter. The deputy confirmed that a tan Chrysler Sebring with a plate starting with the letter was registered to Rita Bowden. Thanking the deputy, Jake hung up. Samantha noted his puzzled expression.

"There was only one car in the garage, Rita Bowden's."

"They were probably keeping the other car you saw for a friend."

"Get real, Sam. They never have anyone over. We've never seen a car in front of the house."

"So why did they have an extra car in the garage?"

"That's what I am trying to figure out," mused Jake.

Their conversation was interrupted by the doorbell. When Sam answered it, Vitello Espennelli was standing there. Apart from facial resemblance and general coloring, Vitello was the opposite of his brother Vinny. Vitello was taller and firmer, though good tailoring probably hid any hint of love handles. A good looking man at least 6 foot 2 and whose body seemed composed of muscle without an ounce of fat, stood behind him.

"Mrs. Lowen? I'm Vitello Espennelli. I wanted to thank you for calling and being there for Leila."

"Please come in."

Speaking to his apparent bodyguard, Vitello said: "Stay with the car, Tony." To Sam, he said: "I would be delighted. I'm a little confused and maybe you could help me make some sense of this unfortunate incident."

Comfortably seated in the living room, the Lowens related the events of the evening at the casino. Vitello listened carefully, occasionally asking a question of clarification.

"So you think Vinny recognized someone?"

"It seems that way, Mr. Espennelli. But whom, we couldn't say."

"Please, call me Vitello. Perhaps it is more important to figure out who recognized Vinny."

"The strange thing is that everyone at the table had their backs turned to Vinny. All eyes were on the man shooting the dice." volunteered Samantha.

"Yet Vinny started over and then hurriedly retreated as though he had seen a ghost?" asked Vitello.

"Exactly. I have been racking my brains to try to figure out who he recognized from the back and moreover, how someone could have recognized him." retorted Jake.

"Well, Vinny could've been caught on a surveillance camera. That can explain his being recognized. But it doesn't explain him recognizing someone else. What else do you remember?" asked Vitello.

"Nothing more than we have said."

"How's Leila today?" asked Samantha.

"Still unconscious. But I doubt if she would be able to give us a name. Vinny didn't involve her in his work very much. She might recognize a mug shot, if the man who did this is known to the cops."

"What you're saying fits in with her telephone call. She told me Vinny came back agitated and told her they were leaving on the first flight they could. He insisted they stay in and use room service. Who would he be so frightened of, Mr. Espennelli, I mean Vitello?" asked Sam.

"I don't know. Only somebody that my associates and I might be looking for and whose whereabouts are unknown to us; if you understand my meaning."

"You and your associates …., you're not involved in the Indian casinos, are you?" Jake was starting to get an idea but needed to test out his theory with Vitello.

"Not really, my associates are connected with the big places in Vegas and Reno, but these tribal casinos are pretty tightly run by the Indians. They don't seem to want our expertise." admitted Vitello.

"So, someone with a gambling habit who for some reason needed to lay low but couldn't do without his or her fix, so to speak, would feel relatively safe from your associates gambling at an Indian casino?" wondered Sam.

"That's correct. Speaking of course in a hypothetical way. If someone wanted to hide out from the elements that have interests in the main casinos, that person would feel safe from observation in an Indian casino."

"But Mr. Espennelli," catching sight of the upraised hand, Samantha continued: "I mean Vitello. If a person was on the run and was found out by Vinny …"

"Then Vinny, may his soul rest in peace, signed his own death warrant."

Jake ventured the idea forming in his mind. "Then the first place to look for Vinny's killer is in the list of people who…have run afoul of your organization."

"Jake, I would appreciate that you not connect me with an organization. It is not healthy for me or for that matter for you. But in theory, if there were an organization, say a group that engaged in various criminal acts, only in theory, mind you, then they might be looking for someone who had done them wrong, so to speak."

"Vitello, when Leila and Vinny were over for dinner, Vinny mentioned Harry Gianelli and how he had stolen twenty million dollars of the mob's money. He also mentioned that Carolyn Gianelli had taken off to find her husband. I can't quite remember if he said that a mobster by the name of Willie the Cook followed her or accompanied her."

"Jake, it's true that Harry Gianelli was a fixer and in deep with the political machine in Cook County. This was in the newspapers, the source of my information. It is also true that Mrs. Gianelli disappeared some days later. I have heard that a certain character named William Carlinski, AKA Willie the Cook, is reputed to have been her traveling companion. It is in question whether Mrs. Gianelli was glad to have Mr. Carlinski's

51

company or he was assigned to her by someone who wanted their money back. The same twenty million dollars that one Harry Gianelli took. You realize of course, that this is merely hearsay on my part."

"Of course, Vitello. We understand that a business man like you comes in contact with lots of people and that various bits of information fall into your lap." said Jake, playing along with Espennelli. "Has anyone heard from any of the parties concerned?"

"There was a rumor that Harry had gone to Vegas where he had a squeeze, but subsequent diligent inquiries failed to turn up any information. It is to Vegas, Mrs. Gianelli was headed. She was seen there looking for her husband. However Mrs. Gianelli and Willie Carlinski have not been heard from for about two months. You understand that this is all hearsay, of course."

"I understand you are not connected to this unfortunate situation, however, your brother did see someone that didn't want to be seen. Would he know any of the people you mentioned by sight?"

"My brother, Jake, wasn't as discriminating in his choice of acquaintances as I would have preferred him to be. He seemed, God rest his soul, to find some satisfaction in associating with undesirable elements. I believe he was on familiar terms with both Mr. Gianelli and Mr. Carlinski. Mrs. Gianelli had been a fashion model, I am sure that Vinny at least knew what she looked like."

"Vitello, what theory do your friends have for the lack of information concerning those missing from Chicago?" asked Sam, reentering the conversation.

"Mr. Carlinski is very skilled in his chosen profession. It's difficult for anyone to believe Mr. Gianelli could have bested him in any conceivable match up. Therefore it is widely assumed that Mr. Carlinski found Mr. Gianelli and the missing money. It is also assumed that the lovely Mrs. Gianelli persuaded Mr. Carlinski to run away with her, using the twenty million as their stake to begin a new life. Mr. Carlinski is known to have a weakness for the ladies and Mrs. Gianelli is quite the lady."

Jake pressed his advantage by asking: "So Vinny might have recognized either Carolyn Gianelli or Willie Carlinski? It would be a very easy task to call around the hotels until one found the one where your brother was staying. Getting the room number might be a little harder; usually the desk doesn't give out room numbers. Carolyn might have dressed in a manner to indicate that she had a professional meeting with Vinny and conned the number from the desk clerk."

"You pose an interesting solution to our little mystery, Jake. I understand you were a history professor and write very interesting books. My wife is a big fan of your Civil War novels. She would love to have her copies autographed by you."

"Thank you, Vitello. I'd be glad to." beamed Jake.

'Do you think you could get some photos of Mrs. Gianelli as well as photos of Mr. Carlinski and Mr. Gianelli?" asked Sam.

'You must understand, Samantha, men in Mr. Carlinski's line of work do not like to have their photos taken. For some reason, in spite of his beautiful wife, Mr. Gianelli was rather camera shy. No good photos exist of either man."

Vitello smoothly changed the subject to his sister-in-law's condition and how, while he would like to wait for her to recover, if indeed she did recover from her wounds, the family had decided to go ahead and hold Vinny's funeral. Vitello was making the arrangements to have Vinny's body shipped back to Chicago. He was leaving a couple of his work associates, Tony, who was waiting by the car, and Larry who was on duty at the hospital, to protect Leila. He profusely thanked the Lowens for their hospitality and for the help they had been in providing some clues to Vinny's murder.

After Vitello Espennelli left, Sam and Jake exchanged notes on his visit.

"I think I need to call Deputy Lodestone, Sam. He needs to be brought up to date on what we have learned."

"What are you thinking, Jake?"

"If Vitello is right, Willie Carlinski caught up with Gianelli and killed him. Of course, there could be three bodies rotting in the desert, you know a three way shoot out like in *The Good, the Bad and the Ugly.*"

"But Jake didn't two of those guys ride away? How about this? Harry and Willie kill each other and Carolyn makes off with the money."

"Or Carolyn kills the survivor of the two and she makes off with the money."

"Jake, we've been assuming it's a man who killed Vinny and nearly killed Leila. What if your idea of how the killer got in is right and it was Carolyn who pulled the trigger? Leila would've been more likely to open the door to a woman, especially if she thought she was delivering room service."

"Sam, I found photos of Carolyn online. If Leila recovers, we can show them to her."

Chapter Twelve

Later that afternoon, Jake reviewed the information he and Sam knew thus far. Arranging them in some order, Jake came up with the salient facts. Harry Gianelli disappears with a large amount of cash. He is followed by his wife and Willie "the Cook" Carlinski, either working as a team or with Willie as a minder of Carolyn. There is the possibility that Carolyn found Harry and some sort of altercation took place. No one, however, seems to know where any of the three are. Vitello indicated that the mob had lost track of all three. Vinny, visiting the Indian casino, recognizes someone and is in fear of his life. The next morning Vinny is murdered. That much was 'fact.'

The big question in Jake's mind is whether these events connected. Is it merely a coincidence that Vinny was relating the disappearance of Gianelli and then is gunned down? Could Vinny have seen someone else who threw him into a state of panic? Jake realized he should have asked Vitello more questions about his brother's associates. Had Vinny crossed someone he shouldn't have? There are too many possible answers. Just like his novels or, for that matter, real life history, there are variant endings that could be written. The historian can only assemble clues, not actually witness the event himself. Depending on the testimony of others has limitations. Were those relating the story actually eyewitnesses? Do they have a particular bent or angle they are approaching the event from? Do they have an 'axe' to grind, a score to settle? Even though he and Samantha had been witnesses to Vinny's panic at the casino, they didn't know the meaning of the event.

At least in the case of Gianelli, there is the corroborating story of Vitello. Vinny, for all his braggato seemed to have gotten the story right. But Jake wondered if he was correct in making a connection between events related by Vinny and his murder. A man like Vinny and perhaps even more so like his brother, Vitello, made enemies. Had Vinny recognized an enemy and tried to get out of the casino before he could be seen? Obviously he hadn't made it.

If Leila survived she might be able to answer some questions. He thought again about how Vitello had posted his own guards at the hospital.

The other nagging question in Jake's mind concerned the extra car in the Rousseaus' garage. Now it's there, now it's gone. Does this have any connection to anything or was it registered in Harold's real name and therefore traceable by his ex-wife who, according to Cindy, is out to get more money from Harold. The easiest way to disappear without leaving a trace is to drive. Airline tickets leave records. Harold, if he was hiding out from his wife, would have driven from wherever he came from. Jake racked his brain to try to remember if Cindy had dropped a clue to where he came from. Vegas was a popular destination for the Southern Californian crowd. Harold reminded Jake of some of the people he had met from the LA area, right down to what Jake now realized was a superior, to-hell-with-you attitude, as though everything and everyone who lived outside the LA basin was a lower life form or at least not important. To be fair, he had met people who lived in New York City who felt the same way about anyone living west of the Hudson River. Regional ethnocentricity, his anthropologist colleagues would call it.

Thinking about Harold Rousseau driving away from his old life made Jake wonder how Harry Gianelli made his getaway. Probably he drove as well. Flying, as Jake had already noted to himself, leaves a traceable record. Anyway, carrying twenty million in cash would trigger suspicion at security. It is too much money to stuff in a carryon and to put it in checked baggage, when current security regulations discourage locked bags, would be a greater risk than Jake would want to take. No, if I were transporting that much money, I would want to drive and also carry a firearm for protection. If there was no APB issued for Harry, he could drive from Chicago to Vegas in three long days, four if he divided the 1800 miles into easily digestible chunks.

Why carry a firearm? Of course, for protection. He would need to bring a gun with him as he couldn't very well go to any of his mob friends in Vegas. They would have sold him out. Given the gun laws, it would be risky to try to buy one at a gun show where he would need to show some kind of ID. Unless he had prepared for his departure by obtaining fake identification, he would need some time to obtain those documents. If I were him, thought Jake, I would try to get a fake passport and leave the country, maybe for Mexico where twenty million dollars could go a long way. I might even want to go farther south, say Argentine. Jake conceded this was all speculation. I don't know what Harry would do or if he even made it to Vegas. If his wife left a week or more later, he might have told her to join him after he got to wherever it was he ended up. Willie the Cook would have complicated Carolyn's escape plan unless he was able to convince her that he was a better protector than her husband. Or perhaps she seduced Willie into helping her. Whatever happened, all three had seemingly disappeared.

Jake pondered over breakfast whether to tell Sam about his dream. It was the second night in a row that the image of the dead woman Jasmine had found appeared to him. She seemed to be asking him for help, but he couldn't understand what she was saying. When Jake awoke, he found himself bathed in a cold sweat with the image of that smashed face still fresh in his mind. Was the woman pleading with him to find her killer? Jake had read up on Lakota History and knew that Dream Catchers were a totem to trap good dreams. He had seen many cars here in the Southwest with Dream Catchers dangling from their rear view mirrors. As Jake pondered the meaning of the dream, he realized he had somehow connected with the murdered woman. But how and who was she? Suddenly, it came to him what to do and his fingers trembled as he dialed the Maricopa County Sheriff Department and asked to be connected to Deputy Lodestone.

"This is Deputy Lodestone, how can I help you?"

"Jake Lowen here. I think I might have a clue to the identity of Jane Doe I found."

"Really, who do you think it might be?"

"One Carolyn Gianelli, wife of a shady character from Chicago with mob connections. She disappeared from Chicago about the right time frame."

"How did you come to your conclusion, Dr. Lowen?"

"It's a bit complicated and involved. You have an internet connection at your desk, don't you? Look up Mrs. Carolyn Gianelli, then try to get a physical description to see if she is the same height and weight of our Jane Doe."

"I'll be glad to follow any lead, but tell me how you came to this conclusion?"

Jake quickly recapped his conversation with Vitello and added the timeframe of Harry Gianelli's disappearance along with Carolyn's search for him.

"Do you think that Vinny recognized Willie Carlinski and Willie killed him?"

"At first I thought it might have been Carolyn who killed Vinny, but the more I think about it, the more I am certain that Sam and I did not see anyone who looked like Carolyn Gianelli at the casino."

"Can you be so sure, Dr. Lowen? After all women can change their appearance fairly easily."

"That's true, and I have used that fact often in my novels. I'm not willing to stake my life on this theory, but I think it's worth checking out."

"So do I. I'll get back to you, Dr. Lowen."

Jake got back to writing his novel and as usual, lost track of time. When he was writing, Samantha had to remind him to eat and Jasmine had to bark to remind him to take her out. So it was several hours later when Jake resolved his problem of saving his heroine when Samantha called to tell him he was wanted on the phone.

"Dr. Lowen, Deputy Lodestone. You could be right on your identification of the body. The forensic guys think it might very well be Carolyn Gianelli. We are contacting her parents to see if we can access her dental records. Her face was pretty badly bashed in, probably to obscure her identity. Based on what you told me, there is another item that might interest you. A car parked in a handicapped space at Sky Harbor Airport in short term parking. The car had Illinois plates, was not sporting a handicap plate or a temporary handicap placard."

"Sounds like it was almost begging to be found."

"It gets better. The ticket for entering the lot was found under the sun visor. It was dated May 29 at 11:56 AM. And the car is registered to William Carlinski."

"11:56! That's the morning Vinny and Leila were shot and the time is right to make it to he airport from their hotel."

"You're right Dr. Lowen, the times fit. But doesn't it strike you as strange that the driver would call attention to the car by parking it illegally?"

"It does, but what if the person was in a hurry?"

"There are plenty of places to park a car. It could be weeks, if not months before a car that is legally parked draws any attention. This is Phoenix. Seasonal residents have been known to leave cars for extended periods, even when there are cheaper and easier parking options. No, this car had the appearance of a car wanting to be found."

"Are there surveillance cameras at the airport?"

"Very perceptive, Dr. Lowen. There are and a review of the tapes shows a man, his face obscured by a hat, getting out of the parked car and heading toward the terminal. We are still checking the camera sequences, but it appears we lost the subject in the terminal. He may have ducked into a restroom and changed his clothes or at least his appearance. But we can't be sure."

"Easy enough to do with a quick change of clothes or even a reversible jacket and baseball cap for the hat he was wearing." volunteered Jake, not revealing that he had used the same stratagem, with period appropriate clothing, in a couple of his novels. "What about departure records?"

"No Willy Carlinski, no Harry Gianelli listed as passengers. Of course he could be traveling on an assumed name."

"We still have the problem of transporting the money and any weapons. Have you checked the car rentals?"

"We have. No rentals in those names, however the video shows a man of average height and build so it is possible that whoever parked the car rented another one."

"It could also be that our illegal parker either took public transport or had an accomplice," volunteered Jake.

"My thought precisely. Checking the cabbies, so far nothing has turned up. It's like he walked into the terminal and then disappeared."

"Maybe he did, Deputy Lodestone, maybe he did." Again Jake remembered his use of the same stratagem in his fiction at least twice, maybe three times. "What about prints on the car?"

"The boys are going over it now, but I'm willing to bet that the wheel and doors have been wiped clean. They hope to turn up something in the trunk. I'll call you when we know more."

Sam wanted to go into see Leila, even though her condition had not changed, so Jake went with her. Vitello's men were still taking turns standing guard on her floor.

"Thanks for coming with me, I feel we should see her, even if she still is in a coma."

"No problem, Sam. Have the doctors said any more about her prognosis?"

"They are still cautious but hopeful that she will pull through. The coma is actually increasing her chances of making it by giving her body time to heal itself."

The visit to the hospital was depressing in that Leila did not show any signs of awareness of her environment, though her vital signs were stable. On the way out of the hospital, Samantha suddenly asked Jake to take her to the casino.

"Feeling lucky or do you just want to have dinner there again?"

"Neither, Jake, though you could talk me into dinner. I really hadn't planned anything for tonight but leftovers."

"Honey, I could eat your leftovers any day, but why do you want to go tonight?"

"Call it a hunch, but we are missing a piece of this puzzle that is at the casino. We just need to figure out what it is."

Chapter Thirteen

rriving at the Talking Stick Casino, Sam and Jake decided to have dinner first. Jake, as ual, was hungry and felt he could think better on a full stomach. Or at least, he claimed, would not be thinking about how hungry he was and therefore unable to devote his full ental energies to thinking about the mystery of who Vinny had seen.

he way I see it, Jake, is that Vinny saw someone he recognized and wanted out of there fore the other person saw him."

Maybe, Sam, but it could be that there was a moment of mutual recognition and some gn passed between them that scared the hell out of Vinny."

You used that in one of your novels, didn't you?"

Yeah, actually in two of them. The two characters see each other and one immediately nows the other is a threat. What builds the tension is the fact that the confrontation can't ccur in the setting where they see each other because of the presence of other people. fter the meeting, however, the one threatened runs for his or her life."

Is there a signal or some sign of recognition that passes between them?"

I used in one novel something very simple. The bad guy moved his finger across his roat."

But we are still puzzled about who Vinny saw when everyone's backs were turned. He asn't even close to the craps table."

Let's have some dessert and coffee, Sam, and then wander over to the gaming tables to ee what we missed. The seven layer chocolate cake looks good."

Jacob Lowen, where do you put all this food and not gain weight? Can I have a couple ites of your cake?" Jake was used to Samantha eating half or more of this dessert, but it nade her even more attractive to Jake.

ater, as Samantha and Jake slowly made their way into the area where they had seen 'inny only a few days before, Samantha suddenly exclaimed, "What dummies we have een. The answer is there on the wall!"

ooking at where Sam was pointing, Jake saw the mirrored surface on the wall. From /here they were standing, they had a perfect view of the craps table and the faces of the layers reflected in the mirror.

Jake, we're about the same place that Vinny was standing when we saw him suddenly ecome frightened. I have an idea. Stay here. I'm going over to the craps table. Watch he in the mirror."

As Jake watched Sam stand at the table, he saw her look up and catch his eye in less time than it takes to relate. She could have been looking at the croupier. In fact, in the mirror Jake saw the croupier look at Sam expectantly. Since she had no chips, she merely shook her head at him.

Rejoining Jake at his vantage point a minute later, Sam said, "Well, what do you think?"

"I think you are a genius, besides being beautiful. You figured it out. Vinny saw someone placing a bet and that person, man or woman, saw Vinny. In that moment of recognition Vinny lost it and hightailed out of the casino."

"Thank you, Jake. But we're no closer to solving the mystery. We still don't know who Vinny saw. Even if it turns out the corpse you found is Carolyn Gianelli, we still don't have a real connection with the Gianelli case and Vinny's murder. This could all be a red herring. Vinny could have crossed someone and that person was nursing a grudge for years. Don't you eastern Mediterraneans do that?"

"We do. But ....wait a minute. These places have surveillance cameras. I wonder how long they keep the tapes."

"Great idea, Jake, but we don't have any standing to waltz in and demand to see their tapes."

"No, but the Sheriff's office does. I wonder if Deputy Lodestone is still on duty."

Lodestone was able to contact the casino office and request that all the surveillance tapes from the evening in question be kept for him to examine. The casino was only too glad to cooperate with the authorities. Anyway, as Lodestone was later to tell Sam and Jake, his cousin was one of the floor managers and made sure copies of the tapes were available for the deputy to review. Because of Sam and Jake's involvement in the case, Lodestone invited them to screen the videos with him in his office the next day.

It was late morning before Lodestone could get everything set up. Reviewing the tapes frame by frame, the trio could see at least ten people who made contact with the croupier during the crucial sixty seconds, determined by looking at another camera angle which caught the expression change on Vinny's face. The particular angle seemed to be coming from behind the mirror wall, a little above the height of the players. It was a wide angle shot, but the technicians were able to zoom in on Vinny's face. From the time markings, they could then go to the other video tapes and find the exact time frames. They reviewed all the camera tapes and were able to isolate which individuals looked up during the crucial time sequence. To be on the safe side, they also reviewed all the tapes from the time Vinny drifted over until after he had left. This was in case he'd been recognized either before or after he recognized the mysterious person who either killed him or had him killed.

"Well, by my count, Dr. Lowen, we have an even dozen possible suspects who looked up during the crucial time sequence."

"That's mine as well. What do you think, Sam?"

"I don't want to be a spoiler, but what if Vinny saw the person in the mirror, but the person never looked up. What if an accomplice of our mysterious gambler saw the whole thing, like we did, and realized Vinny had made an identification?"

"Thanks, Mrs. Lowen. You just made our job a lot harder!"

"Sorry, but we've already speculated that whoever parked Willie the Cook's car at the airport might have had an accomplice, haven't we? Therefore, why not have Vinny spot the person he is afraid of and an accomplice spot Vinny spotting the…, I think you know what I'm trying to say."

"I'm following you completely, Mrs. Lowen, and it makes a lot of sense. But I repeat it still makes our job harder."

"Well, I can see your point, Deputy Lodestone, but we still can identify the person Vinny saw from the frames, even if that wasn't the same person who saw Vinny."

"We don't have any mug shots that we can find of Willie Carlinski. I have contacted the FBI and all they have are a couple of photos taken from a distance with a telephoto lens that might be Carlinski. Our boy was even more camera shy than Harry Gianelli. I will get some help to see if we can match them up to any of the surveillance video." offered Lodestone.

"As much as we think the body Jake found is Carolyn Gianelli, I think we should search the video for anyone who might resemble her. She could have changed her hair style and color. Also, and this is harder, anyone who might look like Harry Gianelli. I know that there aren't many photos of him." suggested Samantha.

"What are you thinking, Sam?"

"Jake, hasn't it struck you strange that the body was so close to the trail in the preserve? It was almost as if it were waiting to be found. If you really wanted to dump a body, there are lots of places where it would stay a long time before it was found, if ever. The smashed face is also suspicious. It could have been done to obscure the woman's features but why leave the body so it could be found. It could be someone else, killed for her resemblance to Carolyn," ventured Samantha.

"Wow! I'm glad you are on my side, Sam. That's a great plot. Anyone reported missing who matches our Jane Doe, Deputy?"

"There are lots of people who go missing every month. Some from their own choice, others are abducted. If our boy, Harry, has been planning this for some time, he could have cultivated a relationship with a woman who looked liked Carolyn for the express purpose of murdering her and making it appear that Carolyn was dead. Willie the Cook would have been an unforeseen problem. Carolyn was probably supposed to join Harry without fanfare someplace and they leave the woman's body as a decoy. Maybe he had even lined up a patsy to take his place. It brings to mind that Steve McQueen movie, *Bullet*, where the bad guy lines up a double to be killed by the mob in his place. Harry may have been planning his exit very carefully with an attention to detail. His frequent trips to Vegas would have given him a lot of time to lay this out and there are plenty of women who might pass for Carolyn, especially if her features were obscured."

Samantha gave an involuntary shudder. "What a wicked man! Not only is he a thief, he's a cold-blooded murderer if your scenario is right, Deputy Lodestone."

"One thing bothers me," injected Jake, "why not head straight for the border?"

"Jake, you told me that yourself and I am certain you have used it in one of your novels. Harry is waiting for three things. One is to establish a new identity. The second is to let things cool down. And, three, if my suggestion is right, is to make it look like he and Carolyn were bumped off by Willie Carlinski who took off with the money. Not only would they stop looking for Harry and Carolyn, they would be looking for someone else altogether."

"Dr. and Mrs. Lowen, you two are certainly bringing up interesting options. Let me see if I can recap our list of suspects. We have either the combination of Harry and his wife, Willie and Harry's wife, Harry, probably with another accomplice and Willie on his own."

"That pretty much sums it up but don't forget to add Willie and an accomplice. We can't neglect the idea that Willie had a woman friend stashed away somewhere. We know that Willie was susceptible to adoring females. Given his line of work, he could have a girl in every major city. Maybe he was tired of being a hit man or had accumulated enough money with or in addition to whatever he scored off Gianelli. He uses Carolyn to find Harry, kills them both, takes the money and contacts his girlfriend to meet him somewhere. She flies in from LA or New York and together they take off for a new life."

"Let me get this straight, Sam. You are suggesting that it is possible that it is Willie that Vinny saw and that his accomplice or more probably girlfriend, saw Vinny seeing Willie."

"That's right, Jake. If Vinny saw someone connected with the Gianelli disappearance then it could be Carolyn, Harry or Willie. Of course, it could be someone else connected with some other event in Vinny's life that he saw, but let's play this one through. We can discount Willie or anyone else acting alone. One of our theories is that whoever parked the car needed an accomplice."

"Mrs. Lowen, if it is Willie, with or without an accomplice, why would Willie draw attention to himself after having successfully gone underground for two months?"

"Because whoever killed Vinny realized that he'd been recognized. Vinny was not a great poker player, his face betrayed his emotions. Let's say it was Willie. He figures, correctly as we know now, that Vinny will call his brother. He needs to act fast. The killer finds out where Vinny is staying, knows it's too late for a flight to Chicago, and bumps him off in the morning. Then the killer either leaves Phoenix or makes it look like he has left Phoenix. Ergo the car parked in a conspicuous location. I don't want to rule out Willie as the murderer. Whether he even left Phoenix is a question mark. I think we are looking for a man and someone else, probably a woman." Samantha paused, as if in thought.

"Sam, I think you are right. According to the profiles of both Harry and Willie, we need to be looking for a woman," declared Jake.

The next few hours were spent examining mug shots and using computer assisted matching in trying to find matches with known felons. It was tiring and tedious work, Jake and Sam were glad to take a break and have dinner with Deputy Lodestone.

"You two have a real knack for police work; ever think about joining the Arizona Rangers?"

"Sorry, I'm retired and Jake has his books to write," laughed Samantha.

"No, the Rangers is a volunteer organization which assists law enforcement as needed. The Rangers must supply their own guns and uniforms but they provide a real service to the community."

"Jasmine and I have already contacted the Scottsdale Company," remarked Jake.

"Let's get back to the task of trying to figure out who Vinny saw."

Several more hours convinced the trio of two things. Since they really didn't know what Willie the Cook looked like, the trio couldn't make any identification from the video. Sam pointed out a couple of women who resembled Carolyn Gianelli, though none who were with a man who looked at all like the grainy photos of Harry Gianelli. Since the women in question were not with a companion, Samantha felt that they should remain on the list of people to be questioned, a judgment with which Deputy Sheriff Lodestone agreed. Before they called it a night, Lodestone had arranged for photos to be made of the potential suspects and for detectives to make discreet inquiries at the casino to find anyone who could identify the individuals from these photos. Lodestone promised to keep the Lowens in the loop if anything developed; Sam and Jake made their way home.

Chapter Fourteen

Leila Espennelli's condition remained critical for nearly ten days. Her bodyguards, supplemented by another team of Vitello's associates guarded her room in rotating shifts. The hospital staff grew accustomed to her guardians. Occasionally if a new nurse came on duty, the bodyguards would politely inquire about this or that drug or treatment, but for the most part they were silent. When Jake and Sam visited, Jake tried not to stare while he checked to see if the guards were packing a firearm. If they were, their tailors were to be commended as the outline of their jackets revealed no visible bulges, though they all appeared to have the physique to excel in hand to hand combat. Since Jake and Sam were on Vitello's approved list, the men were friendly to the Lowens.

On the tenth day, coincidently while Samantha was visiting, Leila came out of her coma and opened her eyes. Struggling to speak, she weakly smiled at Samantha and mouthed a thank you. Sam called the nurse and they were able to get her to suck on an ice chip. Later when Sam spoke with the doctor, he was cautiously optimistic.

"We can't know for certain what she will remember, often the incident is blocked out and the victim has no recollection of the actual event. It is a way of the brain protecting us from reliving the trauma over and over again."

"But she will recover, won't she, doctor?"

"Very likely, the worst is over but her body still needs to heal. She is very weak, but we may be able to start her on soft foods and see how she can tolerate having something in her stomach."

"When do you think she will be up to being questioned by the police?"

"Not for a day or two at the earliest, but as I said she may not remember anything of the attack."

Samantha spent the afternoon holding Leila hand and speaking soothing words, telling her stories of their school days. Leila drifted in and out of sleep, but seemed comforted by Samantha's presence. Her minders had called their boss, who in turn called the Lowen home that evening.

"Mrs. Lowen, I want to thank you for your kindness to Leila. My associates have told me how you have visited nearly every day when she was unconscious."

"It was the least I could do, Mr. …(remembering he preferred to be called by his first name, Sam quickly switched) that is Vitello. How was Vinny's funeral?"

'Lovely, lots of flowers and a big procession to the grave site. Cardinal George sent an auxiliary bishop to say the mass. Vinny got an impressive sendoff. I miss the rascal. He was a lot of trouble sometimes as a kid brother, but …well, family is family."

"That's what my husband, Jake, always says. He is mostly Greek and claims he thinks like a Mediterranean."

Vitello laughed. "I like your husband. He's okay. Now that Leila is coming around, me and some of the boys are planning a trip out. We want to see if she can help us identify who did this terrible thing."

"Please stop by when you get out here."

"It would be pleasure if you would permit me to take you and Dr. Lowen to dinner. They do have a good Italian restaurant in Phoenix, don't they?"

"I am sure they do. It will be a pleasure to see you again."

Later Samantha asked Jake if he would mind having Leila as a house guest for a while after she was discharged from the hospital. Jake readily consented as he found Leila pleasant. It had only been Vinny who got on Jake's nerves.

Discussing the murder of Vinny, Jake asked Sam if she really thought it was connected with Harry Gianelli.

"I think so, but it could be just coincidence. They were here a couple of days before talking about Gianelli's disappearance and the trek west by his wife and a killer to find him. Then, as Vinny said, nothing. I imagine the mob, not to mention the Feds were looking for him in Vegas. The mob was probably also keeping tabs on Willie the Cook. The disappearing act was fairly complete."

"Maybe Leila, when she is stronger, can tell us something," offered Jake.

Two days later, Vitello called from his hotel in Phoenix and asked if the Lowens could join him for dinner that evening. He named a restaurant in Phoenix known for its fine dining, Durant's. He had made reservations and was sending a couple of his associates to pick them up. When Jake protested that he could drive, Vitello indicated that a fine dinner demanded a fine wine. He didn't want Jake to either drive with his reaction time impaired or to forgo enjoying a fine wine. When Jake told Samantha, her only comment was "Wow!"

Right on time, two of Vitello's muscular associates showed up in a Lincoln Town Car. Getting into the vehicle, Jake thought he noticed the curtains of the Rousseau's' house move as if someone was watching them. Mentioning it to Sam when he got into the car, Jake continued. ""Sam, I haven't seen much of the neighbors lately, have you?"

"Are you still looking to catch a glimpse of Cindy?"

Tempted to defend himself, Jake realized that Samantha was putting him on and said instead, "She certainly is a looker. Are you jealous, Sam?"

Provoking a reaction but not the one he wanted, Sam's response was to give him a swift kick in the shin with her high heel.

"Ouch!"

"Anything wrong, Dr. Lowen?" asked Tony.

"No, just an old war wound that gets sore now and then. Thanks for asking."

Dinner was a pleasant affair, Vitello asked about Jake's writing and seemed genuinely interested. He repeated that his wife was a big fan of his novels and was looking forward to meeting him. She had wanted to come on this trip but had to stay home because of some piano recital for the kids. Vitello stated that his wife would come out either when Leila was released or to travel with her back to Chicago when she was well enough.

"Actually that is what I wanted to talk to you about. When Leila is released, could she recuperate at your place until she is well enough to travel? I spoke to the doctor and he thinks that given the nature of her wounds, it would be better not to have her fly or drive home for a couple more weeks."

"Well, we are not exactly equipped to handle someone who has been through what Leila's been through," admitted Samantha with some hesitation in her voice "but we have wondered where she would go to recover."

"Please forgive me. I shouldn't have asked you without notice, but I need to make arrangements on this trip to Phoenix. I know I'm imposing on you. I would pay for round the clock nursing care and my guys would be on guard if you're worried about her and your safety. I know that you would be offended if I offered to pay you, but I really want to make this work and would consider a matter of honor to provide you with a per diem for your inconvenience. If you like, I could hire a cook and a cleaning person to lighten your load. After all, I couldn't expect you to take on all the extra work. My guys would get the groceries and anything else you needed."

"Vitello, that's very kind, if you think she would be comfortable in our home?"

Taking Samantha's hand, Vitello explained, "She trusts you Samantha. Right now it's critical for her healing that she feels safe and is in an environment where she feels love. You won't need to sit with her, just put your head in her room a few times a day. I know of your devotion and how you visited her every day she was in a coma. You needn't tell me tonight. I realize you and Jake need to talk it over. But let me restate that you won't need to worry about anything. I will hire all the staff we need. Consider it a vacation.

ake, you will not be disturbed at all. My guys will park a trailer in the driveway and live out there. Whenever you want to go out, the guys will guard Leila and your house. My guys don't smoke and they are not allowed to drink on duty. The only thing that they might ask is to put a free weight set up in the garage. They are big on staying in shape. Let me repeat, money is not a problem. I will provide everything they need and everything you need as well."

"Vitello, that is extremely generous. But we have commitments and our dog...."

Interrupting Jake, Vitello brushed aside his objections. "Jake, my guys are trained to be discreet and unobtrusive. They love dogs and would be glad to walk her for you. The nurses we would hire would be subject to your approval. Again, consider it like a vacation, no cleaning, no cooking, personal bodyguards round the clock. My family and I would be eternally grateful."

"Vitello, can we consider it?" asked Sam. "I had asked Jake about Leila staying but not with such an entourage."

"Of course, of course. You and Jake talk it over and let me know tomorrow."

On the ride home, Jake confided to Sam that he could get used to be chauffeured around. As they discussed Vitello's offer in the privacy of their bedroom, Jake told Sam that if she felt she owed it to Leila, he was okay with the arrangement.

"It would free me up; I could spend more time in research and writing. And you would get a break from cooking and cleaning for a couple of weeks."

"If it's okay with you, Jake, I would like to help Leila. Maybe she'll remember more of the shooting and can help the authorities apprehend the person or persons who killed Vinny."

"This is a terrible thing to say, and may God forgive me, but with Vinny gone, I think that she might come into her own as a person. He was such a dominating personality that he really quashed her."

"I think you're right, Jake. She has a sweet spirit and Vinny, may his soul rest in peace, didn't appreciate her. Thanks for being willing to help her through this."

Chapter Fifteen

Samantha was busy making preparations for Leila to stay at their home. Vitello had insisted on hiring cleaning staff as well as making provision for a hospital bed to be moved into the guest room that Leila would occupy. Most of the Lowens' furniture in that room would need to go into storage for the duration; again Vitello's associates did the heavy lifting. Jake even got them to move some of his book boxes which saved his back from the strain. Tony and Larry were extremely polite and did their best to be helpful. Certainly destroys the image of callous gangsters, thought Jake. Maybe these are representatives of a newer, more cultivated breed of gangsters. Neither, in spite of their politeness, betrayed any evidence of being soft. If Jake were picking a bodyguard team, these two would head the list of candidates.

Over lunch, Jake asked Sam what was on her mind.

"If there aren't any photos of either Harry Gianelli or Willie Carlinski, how would Vinny have recognized either of them, assuming of course that he saw one or the other?"

"That's fairly easy to answer with regard to Harry. He was a well-known, if not well photographed, figure around the offices of Cook County politicians. And apparently also well-known around the mob. As for Willie, the very nature of his work requires, shall we say, a large measure of anonymity. Presumably the people who hired him would have some contact with Willie, but it's more than likely he didn't frequent the same establishments others did. Vinny could have stumbled on Willie at some time, perhaps even at the site of one of Willie's hits. The fact that he was Vitello's brother would have protected him and at the same time guaranteed his silence."

"But then, Jake, why kill Vinny now, if indeed Willie was the killer?"

"Because Sam, now the stakes are different. Before Willie was on Vinny's side or at least on the side of Vinny's brother. Now, Willie is on his own and not owing loyalty to the mob or anyone else."

Samantha brightened up, "Then Vitello would recognize the photos from the casino."

Jake loved the way Samantha looked when she was pleased with figuring something out and this time was no exception. "Right, but there may be a problem getting Vitello to cooperate with the authorities. The men he works with would like to get the money back, not turn it over to the Feds as evidence for a corruption investigation."

"Hmm. But we could show him photos from the casino, couldn't we?"

"Yes, and land ourselves smack dab in the middle of a Federal probe and possibly be accused of obstruction of justice. The Feds have bigger fish to fry than catching Vinny's killer. They are going after political corruption in the government. Think about it. George Ryan is in prison. Tony Rezco has been convicted. Rod Blagojevich is in prison.

The corruption runs deep and may finally be linked to City Hall. A small time hood like Vinny, no matter who his brother is, is not the big game they are after."

"Are we taking a chance having Leila here, Jake?"

"Not in the corruption probe. There is no way Leila knows anything more about that than we do, I doubt that Vinny confided in his wife that way."

Samantha interrupted Jake, "Leila told me Vinny didn't confide in her. She felt he considered her stupid. She was pretty sure he had a mistress on the side, something to do with his image as a mobster."

"Vinny was obsessed with image. He fancied himself quite the gangster. He told me that he felt undressed without a gun since he couldn't figure out how to get one past security. He actually wanted me to lend him one of mine since he knew I was a collector."

"Jake, you didn't?"

"No, but I have felt guilty about it. Maybe he could have defended himself. But from the description of Leila's wounds, the killer was using her as a shield. With a gun, Vinny might have killed Leila instead of the man behind her."

"Jake, I'm suddenly scared."

"I can understand your fear, honey. But I don't think much will get past Vitello's guards. There is not an army after Leila, only one or two people. Vitello would know if there was a greater danger and make provision."

"It will be strange having her here after Vinny's murder and the attempt on her life."

"Sam, I think Vitello's right. You will be good for Leila. I hate to say it, but maybe being free of Vinny will work wonders for her. Did you see how different she seemed at the Grand Canyon when she was free from under his thumb?"

Samantha laughed. "Vinny was too sick to even lift his thumb, though I still think that was a wicked thing you did, purposely making him carsick."

"You're probably right. But if he made it to heaven, he has forgiven me and if he is in the other place he is too busy trying to quench the burning fires around him to worry about me."

Chapter Sixteen

Jake's was pondering the resolution of a problem in his latest historical novel. His heroine, a beautiful union spy, had fallen in love with a handsome Confederate officer and was uncertain how to proceed on her mission. Stumped, his ruminations were interrupted by the door chime. Knowing Samantha was out grocery shopping, Jake reluctantly turned away from his computer to answer the door. Jasmine, asleep at his feet, only stirred when Jake got up from his desk.

"Some watchdog you are! Burglars could waltz in here and rob us blind if they would only play with you awhile."

Looking sheepish, as if the golden retriever understood the rebuke of her master, Jasmine started furiously barking to alert Jake of someone at the door.

"It's okay, girl. You deserve your rest. Gauging from the way your legs were moving, you were chasing rabbits again. You miss our place in Illinois were you could run around in the fields."

Answering the door, Jake saw three people, two men and a woman. The one man, Jake guessed was his own age, late fifties. He was of average build, about 5' 10" and looked fit. The other two were younger, probably in their thirties. The man was very fit, though not as muscular as Vittelo's associates. The woman was about 5' 6" and extremely attractive with oriental features. They were dressed in business attire and Jake first took them for real estate agents. For a moment, he wondered if they were Mormon missionaries, but they weren't dressed in black suits and white shirts and there were no Bibles in evidence.

"Can I help you?"

"Dr. Lowen?" asked the older man.

"Yes."

Holding up an FBI badge, he continued. "I am Herb Minnelli, Assistant Director, Chicago Field Office of the Federal Bureau of Investigation; this is Special Agent Tom Roberts and Special Agent Holly Tan. We would like to speak to you about an investigation that we are conducting. May we come in?"

"Of course." Quickly Jake went over in his mind his last three tax returns. Surely they can't be coming about his claiming a deduction for the Civil War uniforms and equipment he listed as a business expense. Anyway didn't the IRS audit you first? But still, Jake found his heart racing. Jasmine on the other hand, took an immediate liking to their visitors and accepted the praise and admiration the FBI agents, especially Holly Tan, were lavishing on her.

What a beautiful dog, Dr. Lowen. She looks very intelligent and well behaved. I am a ▪ig fan of goldens myself," volunteered Agent Tan.

'Thank you, she is a great dog. But how can I help you?"

'We apologize for coming unannounced and let me put you at ease right away. We are ▪ot coming in connection with any investigation of you or Mrs. Lowen," offered the older ▪an. "In fact, a friend of yours, Dr. Samuel Johnson, asked me to give you his card."

'How do you know, Sam?"

'We served together in Vietnam and later he helped me solve a case of white collar crime ▪hat also involved murder. You know that Sam is quite the detective?"

'I know Sam and his wife, Judy, as first rate historians. I've heard Sam also sometimes ▪ssists the police. He was a MP in the Army and learned his investigative skills there." Turning the business card that Herb Minnelli had handed him over in his hand, he saw a ▪ote in Sam's handwriting. 'Trust Herb, Jake. Ask him who was the only civilian killed ▪n July 3rd, 1863.'

"Agent Minnelli, I am supposed to ask you who Jennie Wade is."

'Dr. Lowen, Sam wanted to be sure that you knew you could trust me. Knowing you are ▪ Civil War expert, he thought an esoteric question on the Battle of Gettysburg might ▪onvince you that he and I were friends, though you will see that he also wrote his home ▪umber on his business card. Jennie Wade was the only civilian killed during the Battle ▪f Gettysburg. She was baking bread for the Union soldiers, something she had done on ▪he previous two days of the battle, when a musket ball penetrated the door of her kitchen ▪n the morning of July 3rd. She was struck in the head and killed instantly."

"Very impressive, but you could have read it in a book."

Herb laughed aloud. "My reading does not extend to history, I leave that to Sam. I wasn't sure his little bit of information would convince you as my bona fides, but Sam ▪ot quite a kick out of figuring out what question might convince you. Feel free to call ▪im before we continue if you like."

"That's okay, Mr. Minnelli. You certainly have described Sam Johnson. How can I help you?" asked Jake.

"We are not sure you can, but frankly we're at the end of the line with our inquiry and you might have provided a piece of information with the body you found."

"Give credit to Jasmine. She spotted it." At the mention of her name, the dog slightly lifted her ears in the habit of goldens.

71

"She was a search and rescue dog back in Illinois, wasn't she?" The younger man, Tom Roberts, entered the conversation. "Dr. Johnson volunteered that bit of information."

"She was, great nose and dogged determination, if you will excuse the pun."

"We want to talk to you about the body. I was having dinner with Sam and Judy last week and happened to mention that a retired history professor had stumbled onto a corpse we think might have a connection to a case I'm working on. It was only small talk, I hadn't mentioned the case or even your name. It was in conjunction with my comment on how academics like Sam and Judy noticed things. One thing led to another and Sam recalled that a professor he admired for both his teaching and writing had retired to Phoenix for his wife's health. When he mentioned your name, I realized that we were talking about one and the same person. The more we talked, the more I realized that you might know more than you think you do."

"Thanks for the compliment, but I'm still puzzled about how I can help?"

"Your possible identification of the body your dog found as Carolyn Gianelli ties in to an investigation we're conducting."

"You're investigating the disappearance of Harry Gianelli and the twenty million dollars?"

Herb took a deep breath, "It is a bit more complicated than that, Dr. Lowen. If this were a spy story, Harry Gianelli would be a double agent or maybe even a triple agent. Let me begin at the beginning. Harry Gianelli is a mob fixer. He would bribe government officials to offer contracts to his clients. Most of his clients were mob owned businesses that wanted a place to launder money. Some were contractors controlled by the mob. They had been forced to 'sell' part of their business to the mob for the privilege of staying in business. Those who refused to make the mob their silent partner found themselves the victim of all kinds of trouble: mysterious fires, equipment damage, labor problems. If they still held out, the violence escalated to injury to their families. Some turned to us for protection and that was how the bureau got involved. The local authorities either turned a blind eye or were being paid off not to intervene. The few investigations that did take place were cursory. When I pressed the investigating officers, they spoke of pressure coming down from above to go easy."

Jake let out a low whistle. "This is serious stuff, though from my reading of history, fairly typical Chicago style politics."

"'Fraid so. But we are trying our best to clean things up. That is where Harry Gianelli fits in. He was caught in a sting operation we were running and we had him dead to rights. But as big as a fish as he was, we thought we could use him to get to the corrupt politicians as well as the mob. The deal was that he would turn state's evidence and name names. If the convictions stood, we would provide him with a new identity and put him into the witness protection program. His reward was dependent on making the case

72

tick. We didn't want him to weasel out at the last minute and walk with a guarantee of immunity."

"Did his lawyer buy that? Wouldn't he have insisted on some promises to his client?" queried Jake.

"Harry doesn't trust anybody, least of all any lawyer in the pay of the mob. He knew that everybody has a price or can be frightened into cooperating with the mob. That is not strictly true; there are honest people out there, our mutual friend, Sam Johnson, is one of them. And from what he tells me, so are you, Dr. Lowen. But Harry Gianelli doesn't know any."

Their conversation was interrupted by Samantha's voice coming from the kitchen. "Can you help me with the groceries, honey?" Entering the living room, Sam said: "Oh, I didn't know we had company."

Introductions were made all around and Tom Roberts volunteered to bring in the groceries for Samantha while Jake took the opportunity of a break in the conversation to make coffee. Holly asked if she could take Jasmine outside to play.

Waiting for the Tom and Samantha to finish, Herb commented on the view. "Lovely place you have here, Dr. Lowen. Sam said you moved out here for your wife's health."

"Yes, we did. But I had enough time in to retire and retain my benefits and writing both novels and historical studies started to look more attractive than continuing to teach."

Herb continued, "Tom won't admit it, but he is addicted to your Civil War novels."

When they were rejoined by the others they repaired to the dining room. Samantha served a coffee cake she conveniently had bought. Tom asked about the Lowens' life back in Illinois. Herb, however, cleverly steered the conversation to the Lowens' friends, particularly Leila and Vinny Espinnelli. Jake saw it coming; he had wondered when Samantha's friend would come into play.

"So Vinny told you about Harry Gianelli?"

"Yes, but not with the detail you were sharing before Samantha returned. Why don't you pick up the story where you left off, Herb?" Jake and Herb had resorted to first names during the coffee break.

"Where was I? Oh, that's right. I was talking about our deal with Harry. We were going to offer him conditional immunity from prosecution. As you so perceptively asked, no lawyer would have bought it, but Harry acted as though he had no choice. He was playing us all the while, figuring to make his escape. He told our guys that he was making another trip for the mob and would come back with more evidence. He slipped his minders and got away."

73

"You had a tail on him?" asked Samantha.

"We had him in our sights all the time. He is a valuable asset that we wanted to protect. Our guys, Tom and Holly, as part of the surveillance team, noted the presence of someone else tailing Harry."

"The mob?" interrupted Samantha.

"We are pretty sure it was. They brought in some out-of-towners to work with their own boys, not wanting Harry to spot one of his own on his tail. In spite of our efforts, he shook us off at O'Hare and hightailed it out of town. We think he went to Vegas, he apparently had a girl friend there, to lie low. But the mob turned the town over looking for him, saving us the trouble. They couldn't find him. This was after they sent Willie Carlinski, AKA Willie the Cook, after him with his wife."

"Was his wife part of the witness protection deal?" asked Samantha.

"Harry wanted her to be, or at least that's what he told us. But he wouldn't let us talk to her. Was afraid she might talk or somehow give the plan away. Insisted on playing his cards close to his chest, our boy Harry did. Right now, Harry has disappeared, Carolyn has disappeared and Willie has disappeared. We don't know where any of them are. Willy is a ruthless killer, he could have gunned down Harry, Carolyn and Harry's Vegas squeeze without thinking twice. He might be tempted to clear out with the twenty million without checking in with his bosses. On the other hand, Willie is a ladies' man; he could have linked up with either Carolyn or Harry's Vegas girlfriend. Or be holed up with yet another female companion who he is using to run his errands until the heat is off."

Samantha inquired, "When will the heat be off, Agent Minnelli?"

"Please call me Herb. From our side, not for a while. We are seriously trying to wrap up this prosecution of corruption in Illinois. The stuff we've done so far, former Governor Ryan, Tony Rezco; this is just the beginning. Chicago has been rife with corruption; we would like to make a serious dent in it. However, from the mob's side, probably never. They have long memories; those guys need to catch Harry as an example to others."

"It will be great if you can begin to clean up Illinois politics. We would applaud you for that. But where do Samantha and I fit in? We weren't exactly friendly with the mob or the politicians. The last Illinois politician I feel I know intimately was Abraham Lincoln. Don't get me wrong, I vote and I want my vote to count, but only so much comes out before the election, if it comes out at all. And after the election, they seem to be serving their own interests and those of their cronies. How can we help you?"

"Well, for starters, you found a suspicious body that you suggested to the sheriff's department might be Carolyn Gianelli. Then you assisted in trying to figure out who Vinny might have seen. And third, Vitello has asked you to have Leila stay with you while she recovers. That pretty much puts you in the middle of things, wouldn't you say?"

"Herb, you make some good points. Was the body identified as Carolyn's?"

"Her folks made a positive identification, but we aren't so sure. We think that they are somehow aware of Carolyn's desire to get away with Harry, in spite of what Harry said about not talking to Carolyn about his plans. Actually, what he said was he didn't want us to talk to Carolyn. For all we know, she was in on it from the start. We had to release the body for burial but we still think that it might not have been Carolyn who they buried. We are still waiting for the DNA testing for a positive confirmation."

"Do you think that they just wanted closure?" asked Jake.

"That is a possibility, they wanted to be able to grieve. But Holly was at the funeral, in disguise as one of Carolyn's friends from her modeling days and she's not sure about the parents."

"But if Harry and Carolyn planned to disappear, Willie's coming along messed up their plans." Samantha was obliviously curious.

"Harry is such a wily bird; he may have counted on the mob coming after him and hoped it would be Willie. Maybe Willie was in on it, though that is doubtful, or was recruited by Carolyn on the trip, which is more probable. We are working on the assumption that all three or any combination of the three are still alive."

"One of the problems that Deputy Lodestone faced was the absence of good photos of Harry." mentioned Jake.

Tom spoke up again, "We can rectify that, we have some good candids we took when we were doing a surveillance of Harry," as he spread out several 8 x 10s on the table.

Looking them over, both Jake and Samantha shook their heads at their lack of recognition.

"One of the problems is that Harry was an actor before he took up being a fixer. He's an expert at makeup and apparently was quite good at amateur theater in college and in some community theater productions. He may have altered his appearance by appearing to have put on weight, change his hair color and style, even alter his eye color with contacts," continued Tom.

"How else do you think we can help, Herb?" asked Samantha.

"I am glad you asked; meet your niece, Holly, from New Jersey. She is your sister's eldest daughter out for a visit and looking to start a new life. Holly is going through a nasty divorce and needs to be away from New Jersey for a while. Holly asked if she could stay with her favorite Aunt and Uncle. Holly will be able to keep tabs on your house guests and see if anything else is going on. She knows Harry by sight, but we never let Harry meet Holly in her real capacity or any capacity for that matter. She really is from New Jersey, works in our Newark office. For the record, she is single, not really going through a divorce, but has been prepped on how she should act and talk as a divorcee including how to both attract the muscle Vitello is bringing in and put them off with phrase like, 'it's too soon,' or 'I'm not ready to get serious again and I don't want to fool around.'"

"Wow, this place is going to get crowded. I'm glad we have the room!" exclaimed Jake.

Entering the conversation, Holly spoke up. "I realize that this is an imposition, but it might help crack this case. The bureau has worked so long with the Justice Department to clean up corruption. We know that we won't get it all, but it has to start somewhere. I promise not to get in the way of your writing Dr. Lowen, that is Uncle Jake. And Jasmine and I are already starting to bond."

Samantha asked, "When will you want to move in?"

"Tomorrow, if Uncle Jake could collect me from the airport. I need to perform a little makeover in case any of your neighbors were watching when we pulled up. I want to be settled before Leila is released next week and establish a routine so that the neighbors are accustomed to me."

"Holly, you are most welcome. It will be fun to have a niece around for awhile. Would you like to go a spa with me? The last time I took Jake he bought a box of books while I was getting a facial."

"That would great Samantha. It would increase my cover story while I get pampered at the department's expense."

Herb interjected, "Hey, easy on the budget." But it was said with a smile.

After their guests left, Sam and Jake compared notes.

"Well, we certainly have stepped into it now, you and your uncanny ability to find dead bodies, Jake. Look where it has gotten us."

"Hey, that's not fair. Most of the bodies I find are over a hundred years old and died in America's bloodiest conflict. It's not like I make a habit of turning over corpses every day. Anyway, it was Jasmine who discovered the body. Besides we would be involved in spite of the body. It was your friend, Leila and her husband who really got us into this mess."

"That's true, Jake, I'm sorry. I just don't know if I can cope with all the people running around the house. Fortunately, we have guest bedrooms as well as your study."

76

"Remember, Samantha, we chose this house in part for the view but also because of the layout. The guest rooms are in the other wing so company wouldn't disturb my work or our sleep."

"You're right, they can have the guest wing as we may as well call it and we will be separated from them by the family room, dining room, living room and kitchen. This is a great floor plan." The Lowens' home was in the shape of a U, with one arm of the U housing the guest wing, the other the master bedroom and Jake's study. The family room, living room, dining room and kitchen stretched across the back of house in an open great room style.

"Obviously devised by retirees who wanted their kids and grandkids to visit but wanted some privacy of their own as well, Samantha. The only thing I'm worried about is that Jasmine will be spoiled by all the attention."

"You and that dog, Jake. I swear you worry about that dog more than you do me!"

Taking her in his arms and planting a kiss on her lips, he said, "You know that isn't true, but you also know that saying it will get you a hug and kiss."

Chapter Seventeen

Jake was busy in his study, puzzling as usual over a conundrum in his latest novel when the doorbell rang. Jasmine, more alert than yesterday, gave a low growl to alert him of someone in the driveway.

"I'll get it, Sam," called out Jake as he strolled toward the door. Opening to the UPS man who asked for his signature for the delivery, he was startled by the UPS guy's greeting.

"Good morning, Dr. Lowen." The UPS man spoke quietly and quickly. "Herb wanted to be sure you got this package before picking up Holly at the airport. Please open it and take it with you in a briefcase. Of course, it goes without saying that the contents should be left in the car and not taken inside the airport."

"Tom, are you moonlighting or is it just a disguise the Bureau adopts at times when they are on surveillance?"

"The latter. Just so you're not surprised, the box contains Holly's firearms and her shield. She is actually arriving on a flight this afternoon from Denver and wanted to be sure she didn't have to declare anything like a firearm in her checked baggage or have her shield picked up in the X-ray of her hand luggage. Herb also suggested you might want to carry yourself while your guests are here. Nothing to worry about from Vitello's boys, but there's still the possibility someone will make another attempt on Leila Espennelli's life. Unlikely, but Herb doesn't want to take any chances. He wants you two to treat Holly like your favorite niece and take her around. Make sure she is visible to your neighbors in the street, let her walk Jasmine or better yet, walk Jasmine with her for a few times and then let her do the duty. This operation depends on her passing herself off as a relative. If Samantha has the opportunity, let her have the women in neighborhood for coffee to meet Holly. It will also give her the opportunity to get the word out that Leila will be coming to recuperate. How are you going to explain the bodyguards?"

"Well, we thought we would say Leila's family is well off and can afford private duty nurses round the clock. The men are trained physical therapists from her husband's business, which we are saying was a health club, they are here to help get her muscle strength back. Apart from the fact that Vinny never stepped inside a health club, let alone owned one, the rest of the story is plausible since we're not hiding the fact that Leila was shot in the attack that killed her husband."

"How are you handling the murder, Jake?"

"We are sticking as close to the truth as possible. It appeared to be the work of someone trying to get Vinny to sell his business. Vitello is okay with turning the tables and saying it was a mob related hit on his brother, an honest business man. Speak well of the dead seems to be his motto."

"And use the dead for his own purposes, eh, Jake? Tell Holly hello for me. I will be in the background providing cover. Herb will be in and out, he needs to cover the Chicago office."

After Tom left, Jake unwrapped the parcel. Inside were two firearms, one he recognized as the FBI standard duty weapon, a Smith & Wesson .40 caliber semiautomatic pistol. Jake remembered this caliber was adopted after the disastrous shoot-out in Miami in 1986. The FBI had been on the trail of two savage bank robbers for six months and the confrontation on April 11 changed the tactics and the armament of the Bureau. In a nutshell, the FBI was outgunned by the robbers who were armed with a variety of weapons. The criminals had managed to kill or wound all six agents before finally being put out of action. That gunfight is compared by some to the shootout at the O.K. Corral in 1881 when Wyatt Earp and his brothers, aided by Doc Holiday took on the Clancy gang.

Hefting the pistol, Jake went over in his mind the evolution of the handgun and how it had become the weapon of choice for law enforcement in their attempt to match the lethal weapons of their adversaries. He also wondered if when this was over he could get one of the special agents to accompany him to a pistol range so he could try out their duty weapon. The 9mm pistols that the agents had carried into the gunfight did not have the stopping power needed to bring the encounter to a quick conclusion. The upgrade to the larger caliber with its heavier bullet was an attempt to balance power with firepower as the .40 magazines held more than the older .45 caliber pistols. Jake chuckled as he remembered his friend, Sam Johnson, and Sam's preference for a .45 caliber 1911 service pistol. Jake determined to call Sam before he left to pick up Holly.

The other weapon in the box was obviously Holly's backup gun, a Smith & Wesson, Model 340PD Revolver in .357 Magnum. Mindful of Tom Robert's admonition to load both and take them to the airport, Jake set about his task. He admired Holly's choice of armament and wondered how proficient she was. He knew that agents needed to qualify regularly with their service weapons and made a mental note to ask her about the procedure.

Since there was still time before leaving for the airport, Jake decided to take a chance and see if he could get Sam Johnson on the phone. Dialing the number on the card, he reached Sam's office only to be told by his personal assistant that Dr. Johnson was tied up for the day in meetings, but promised to pass on Jake's message and ask Sam to call Jake.

Later in the morning, lingering over coffee with Samantha, Jake went over their back story to explain Holly's presence with them.

"Holly is your sister's daughter, right Sam?"

"Yes and her dad is second generation Chinese American which explains her surname. She is readopting her maiden name in the aftermath of her divorce."

"We better ask her what name she is going to use for the non-existent divorced husband. No kids, right?"

"No kids, Jake. Husband a philanderer, marriage lasted slightly less than two years from the part of the cover story we went over yesterday. I think I have the story down, just forgot to ask for the non-existent husband's name."

"The man with no name, that would be a great title for a book or a movie."

"Already taken, as you well know, Jacob Lowen. The movies starred Clint Eastwood as the man with no name and there are at least a half dozen novels using that title."

"Always room for one more, Samantha. I could write one for each historical period starting with the Civil War and moving to the present."

"Why not earlier?"

"Sam, you know we historians have our areas of specialization. I would need to research the colonial period and you know that means more books to buy. You said you wanted me to cut back on my book purchases."

"Cut back is an understatement; we are already out of space on your bookshelves!"

"I can always build more bookshelves; there's still room to expand."

"Jake, you are incorrigible, which is one of the many things I love about you. Come on, let's get going. It is almost time to pick up Holly.

Chapter Eighteen

On the way to the airport, Samantha and Jake discussed how their lives were going to change with house guests, first Holly, then when Leila was released with her nurses and bodyguards. They agreed that Jasmine would love the extra attention and realized that they were virtually giving up the use of the guest wing of their home.

"Thank God we have the space; you won't be bothered in your writing, Jake."

"I agree, but maybe if we didn't have the space, we wouldn't be in the middle of this ness."

"Jacob Lowen, you were the one who wanted a bigger place to be able to have your books."

"True, but we both agreed that we wanted to have space to have the kids and grandkids visit and we managed to accomplish both goals. Anyway, this will give me more characters to use in my writing."

"Are you going to park?"

"I think so, after all, Holly is our favorite niece. But I'll drop you by the door so that you won't have to walk as far."

"Jake, do you think that the FBI will have some agents around?"

"They don't want to risk valuable assets. I think you can count on it, Sam. Or should I start calling you Aunt Samantha?"

"You mean risking Holly?"

"I mean risking you and me, Sam. We are the best pipeline they have right now. I think Herb Minnelli suspects the hit on Vinny is somehow connected to Gianelli's disappearance. Actually, so do I."

"Will they have the house under observation, Jake?"

"Only very discreetly. That's why they are embedding Holly with us. It means that they have an agent in place. 'An Agent in Place,' that would make a great book title."

"Jake, you know darn well there are at least three paperbacks with that title, though I think the one by Helen Macinnes doesn't have the definite article and is only called *Agent in Place.*"

"Bonus points if you can name the other two authors, Sam."

"Robert Littell and Thomas Whiteside both wrote books with that title."

"You're good Samantha."

"Thank you, am I correct?"

"I don't know," admitted Jake, "I only knew of the Macinnes book, which unlike most of her others, doesn't have a romance at the center of the book."

"How much have you gotten inspiration from all your reading, Jake?"

"I don't know. As one of my professors in graduate school said, 'to borrow from one source is plagiarism, but to be indebted to hundreds of sources is creativity.'"

"Do you buy that?"

"I don't know, Sam. I just know that I have wanted to write every since I was a kid. All our experiences and all my reading and study have just added details to my desire to tell stories."

"You're being too modest, Jake. I know you give proper acknowledgement of your debt to other writers and cite any work you've quoted, even in your novels."

"That's true. Plagiarism is one of the things that really sets me off. In most cases it is symptom of laziness at best and stupidity as worst, with a criminal disregard for intellectual property in-between. I was relentless on my students when I caught them plagiarizing. The internet and the software solutions our IT guys put in place really help catch them. What really got my ire, and in fact still does, is when a professor or an administrator plagiarizes. I was for punishment when those cases came up before the Faculty Personnel Committee. There was that highly publicized case in New York where a professor was found to have plagiarized passages from the dissertations of students she had supervised. But what does this have to do with what we are involved in now?"

"Jake, I think that this case involves a plagiarism of persons. Somehow it seems to revolve around people copying other peoples' identities. But I haven't figured it out as yet. Maybe plagiarism isn't the right word, but it involves more than just identity theft. In identify theft, people just steal your information, here I think it is case of someone actually assuming the life of another person."

"Sam, I think I am following you. Someone has taken the identity of Carolyn and Harry?"

"Something like that, or more likely Harry and Carolyn have assumed the identity of someone else. People aren't who they seem and I think that Vinny stumbled on the identity switch. He may not have realized what he was seeing, but his killer couldn't take a chance."

"You mentioned something like this when you were identifying or rather trying to dentify the body that Jasmine and I found."

'I did. I admit that I thought the body was Mrs. Bowden, but I was wrong. I just can't quite get it. I am not sure who is who."

'Certainly at least we can eliminate Mrs. Bowden."

'Can we, Jake? After all how well do we know her? What a perfect place to hide, an orphanage in Thailand with an assumed identity."

'Are you suggesting that Mrs. Bowden isn't who she says she is in the postcard?"

'Not really Jake, but I'm only pointing out how easily a person could switch identity. Suppose you wanted to disappear and found someone who looked like you. Isn't there a theory that everyone has an exact double running around somewhere in the world."

"That theory is widely held in folk cultures, but its scientific basis is not as secure. The mathematical odds are virtually impossible for an exact double, though obviously there are people who look like other people, discounting of course those who are related to each other. There are people who are adopted who were separated at birth or while young children who don't have a memory of a sibling. Then there are the cases of identical twins who were raised separately who, when reunited, discover not only do they look alike but have similar tastes in music, etc. The actual word 'doppelganger' comes from the German and in folklore meant a spirit or wraith that was the person's double. The doppelganger did not cast a reflection in a mirror and it was considered a sign of imminent death to meet your doppelganger. However, the word has come to mean what you were calling an exact double. Some use the term to just mean someone who looks like you, just like the scientific word 'clone' is used to designate someone with common characteristics, like friends who think alike."

"Thanks for the lecture, professor, but I think you've caught my drift."

"Sorry Sam, you know how I tend to lecture at the drop of a hat."

Laughing, Samantha said, "That's okay. You can take that professor out of the classroom but you can't take the professor out of the man. Anyway, you save me a lot of time that I would waste looking stuff up in an encyclopedia."

"You're only saying that to be nice to me and because you know I've written a lot of encyclopedia articles. But you seriously think this case hinges on look-a-likes?"

"I do and I won't be surprised to find out there are more doppelgangers running around than we might have suspected.'

Dropping Sam at the arrivals level, Jake was able to quickly find a parking spot. Since they weren't going through security, he slipped Holly's badge and revolver in his backpack and headed for baggage claim. They arrived early and so were able to meet Holly as she came up to the carousel. For all observing the scene, it was just like family members greeting a well loved relative. Jake helped Holly retrieve her bags and they headed out to the minivan. Once in the van, the trio felt able to discuss their true mission

"I'm glad you had a good flight, Holly. Are you hungry?" asked Samantha.

Before Holly could reply, Jake chimed in, "I hope you are, because I'm hungry."

"Jake, you're always hungry. Don't mind him; he's mostly harmless except at feeding time when it's dangerous to get your hands too close to his mouth."

Laughing, Holly asked, "When's feeding time?"

"With Jake, all the time is feeding time!" Turning to Jake, Sam said, "Sorry honey, that was too good to miss."

"It's okay Sam, in humor, romance and hunting, timing is everything and your timing on that was great."

From the backseat, Holly commented, "I think I'm going to enjoy this assignment. You two are a lot of fun. How long have you been married?"

"Thirty-five years of marital bliss or something that passes for it," volunteered Jake.

Again Holly broke into laughter.

"Seriously, we should grab some lunch. What do you fancy?"

"I would like to get settled first and stow my bags, but one of the priority items to see is the casino."

"If sandwiches are okay for lunch, why don't we have dinner at the casino, if that okay with you, Jake?"

"Sounds good, Sam. I would be happier with Holly's luggage out of the car and she is back in possession of her shield and gun."

Leaving Holly to get settled, Sam prepared lunch while Jake took Jasmine for a short walk. As they were passing the Rousseau's house, Cindy was pulling in. She stopped to say hi to Jake and Jasmine.

"My wife's niece from New Jersey is out for a visit; she is going through a painful divorce and is thinking about moving out here. It would be nice for you two to meet. Would you like to come over for coffee later this afternoon?"

Jake could see the hesitation on Cindy's face, as though she didn't want to get involved. It was suddenly replaced by another look that Jake couldn't quite figure out. "I'd love to. What time?"

"About three?"

"Perfect, see you then."

Watching Cindy park her car in the driveway and go through the garage door she had opened with a remote control on her sun visor, Jake wondered why Harold parked his car in the garage and made Cindy park outside. Call me old fashioned, thought Jake, but I would let Sam park her car in the garage and leave mine outside, especially since she seems to be doing all the shopping and errands. Come to think of it, Jake realized that he had not seen Harold outside of the house for several days, while Cindy seemed to be in and out at least once a day, usually more often.

Entering the house, he found Holly and Samantha working together in the kitchen getting lunch. They will do well together, mused Jake. Over lunch he informed the women of his invitation.

"Great work, honey. I was hoping to get Holly to met Cindy."

"Is there a special reason you wanted me to meet her, Samantha?"

Before she could answer, Jake said. "Sam has this idea that Cindy and Harold aren't who they claim to be…"

Interrupting, Samantha continued. "Jake is making fun of me, but I think there's something strange about Harold and Cindy. She claims he is hiding out from his first wife who is after him for more money in the divorce settlement. But I think, and if Jake is honest with you so does he, there's something fishy about her story."

"Actually, Holly, I do agree with Samantha. Cindy looked like she was on the verge of begging off when her countenance suddenly changed and she agreed to come."

"Sounds like an interesting couple. What's my role?"

"Maybe you can suggest doing something with Cindy to get to know her. You are closer to her age and if she is telling the truth, she might want to hear about your divorce."

"Then we better work on the story to be sure we have at least the basic facts straight."

Chapter Nineteen

During and after lunch, Jake and Samantha filled Holly in on their visits to the casino, including the night before Vinny was murdered. Holly expressed a desire to see the area for herself. Anyway, she said she was feeling lucky and might wager a little money on some of the games. When Sam looked puzzled, Holly confessed it was just a way to hang around the casino without attracting too much attention. People who don't gamble stand out at casinos she explained. The trio made plans for Leila's arrival which looked to be in about a week. That would give time for Holly to settle in and check out the area. She was particularly interested in seeing the area where Jasmine found the body. After an orientation to the neighborhood, she planned on checking in with the local office through Tom who would be her liaison and looking over the police files on both the woman's body as well as Vinny's murder.

Promptly at three, the door bell chimed and Samantha admitted Cindy Rousseau. Before disappearing to his study, Jake couldn't help but notice that Cindy seemed to have dressed down for her visit as she was considerably less formally dressed than when Jake had seen her earlier in the day.

Later, as Samantha related the story of the coffee time to Jake, she mentioned that both women shared their stories. Cindy's was consistent with the story she had told the Lowens before, though she discreetly omitted any reference to Harold's outburst of temper or of any fear she had of him. For her part, Holly elaborated on the background she was using of a bad marriage and a chance at a new start in the west. The presence of her favorite aunt and uncle seemed to be a combination too good to pass up. Cindy concurred and mentioned how she longed for a new start from her old life and how she hoped to achieve that goal with Harold if his ex-wife would stop looking for him. Holly, her legal training on high alert, honed in on this.

"The divorce is nearly final, but she's still trying to bleed him for more money. That's why we are hiding out, so to speak. He doesn't want her to find us."

"But Cindy, if Harold had so much money, why didn't he hire the best divorce lawyer he could find?" asked Holly. "That's what I did."

"Harold had a good lawyer, but his wife's lawyer brought up the lifestyle issue, keeping her in the style to which she had become accustomed and the judge bought it."

"I am sympathetic with you, Cindy" interjected Samantha, "but surely there they could have reached a fair settlement. I knew a couple where the husband had divorced his first wife. He was from a wealthy family and settled property on her quite fairly. Then after a few years, the husband married again. The first wife came after him for more money more than ten years after the divorce. I don't know all the details, whether she had something on the husband or he just had a soft heart for the mother of his children, but he gave her another $2 million because she had run through the millions she received at the divorce."

"Wow! What happened?" asked Cindy with wide eyes. Holly was following Samantha's story with obvious interest.

"It's a very sad story. After the settlement with the first wife, the second wife, who was about 15 years younger, met someone else and asked for a divorce. Jake knew the husband quite well and he was the nicest guy. He apparently had poor taste in choosing women."

After Samantha finished, there was an awkward silence. "Oh, dear. I'm sorry. I didn't mean to imply anything by my story. I apologize for offending either of you."

Holly was first to speak. "No problem, Aunt Samantha. I'm not offended. I made a wrong choice. Mom and Dad tried to warn me, but you know how headstrong I can be. I just want to learn from this and move on. It has made me want to study law though."

Cindy, still lost in thought, managed to mumble, "It's okay, Samantha. These things happen and we do need to learn from other's mistakes as well as our own. That was one thing I learned on the stage."

Thinking of how to change the subject, Samantha thought about mentioning Leila's convalescence and was puzzling about how to bring it up when Holly beat her to it.

"Aunt Sam tells me that we are having another house guest, isn't that right?"

"Yes, an old school friend of mine was wounded in the attack that killed her husband right here in Phoenix. She is being released from the hospital in a few days."

Cindy's eyes widened. "A murder! Here in Phoenix! How terrible!"

Sam, taking Holly's cue, proceeded with the story. "She and her husband were visiting. Jake and I had spent a day with them, driving to the Grand Canyon. Leila, that's the wife, and I had a spa appointment the day they were attacked. Apparently they ordered room service and the killer slipped in pretending to be the waiter. The real waiter came up later with breakfast and when no one opened to his knock called the front desk to ask them to ring the room. When they got no answer, they unlocked the door and found my friends. The husband died on the scene, but the wife survived. It was touch and go, but she made it and will be recovering here. Maybe you read the story in the paper, Vinny and Leila Espennelli from Chicago?"

Cindy visibly blanched. "Oh, my God!"

"Are you okay, Cindy? Can I get you some water? You look like you are going to faint." enquired Holly with a solicitous tone in her voice.

Gasping for breath, Cindy stammered. "It's just that …I abhor violence. Living in Vegas … there was so much … I'm sorry. I'll be all right. Just give me a second."

Pressing her advantage with an obviously troubled Cindy, Holly continued. "The authorities think that Leila will be able to identify her assailant when they can question her at length. Apparently she opened the door to the killer who used her as a shield while gunning down her husband. Then the killer tried to kill Leila, but the shots missed the vital organs by a hair. They think having her in a friendly environment will help her recover more quickly than in a hospital."

"But will she be safe here? Won't the killer try to eliminate her as a witness?"

"Her husband's brother runs a health club. He is, of course, anxious to help the police find his brother's killer. He is sending out a team of physical therapists to work with her. They will be living in a trailer which will be parked in our driveway. She will also have round the clock nurses. She won't be alone. And of course, Jake and I will be here and Holly is our guest for as long as she likes," added Samantha, giving Holly's hand a squeeze as she smiled at her niece.

"Oh! Well, that should be all right." Glancing at her watch, she said: "Look at the time, I must be going. Thank you so much for the lovely afternoon. Holly, it was nice meeting you. Maybe you and I can have lunch sometime and talk about starting over."

"That would be great, Cindy. I would like to meet Harold."

"Actually, we would need to eat out, I am not much of a cook and Harold doesn't like to have company. He is really nervous about his ex finding out where he is."

"I hear there are some great places to eat in Phoenix. How about tomorrow at 11:30?"

Cindy paused for a moment, as if considering her social calendar. "Yes, I think I can make it, I'll drive. Pick you up at 11:30. Thank you again, Samantha. See you tomorrow, Holly.

After she left, Jake joined them as he was heading for some coffee and a snack himself.

"Jacob Lowen, you will spoil your dinner!"

"Samantha, you know that I can eat anytime. How did it go?"

"Holly is a very clever detective. I was trying to figure out how to bring up the subject of Leila staying here when she plunged right in."

"Did you notice how her countenance changed when I introduced the murder, Samantha? She nearly went white."

I did, Holly. Do you buy the story about her seeing so much violence in Vegas?"

"Not really. Chicago has nearly three times the national average for murders, though those are concentrated in certain gang-infested areas. Vegas only has slightly more than one and half times the national average. If you look at crime statistics, it isn't so bad, though car thefts and burglary are both higher. But murder, no. D.C. is the murder capital of the country with over five times the national average. I think our friend has seen more of the underside of life than she is letting on."

"Brilliant of you to ask her to lunch. What do you hope to learn?" asked Samantha.

"I want to hear more of her story and see if I can figure out what's going on."

"Do you suspect something?" asked Jake.

"Call it my intuition or my instinct, whatever, Cindy's story has something wrong with it."

"What time would you lovely ladies like to go the casino tonight?"

Chapter Twenty

"Wow, I'm sure getting the looks from everyone, escorting two beautiful ladies."

"Jake, you old flatterer, you know everyone is looking at Holly. You look lovely this evening, Holly."

"Thank you, Aunt Samantha, but you are selling yourself short. You are a very attractive lady and you and Jake make a handsome couple."

"Got that right, Holly. Samantha is always giving me a hard time about how I manage to maintain my slim, trim figure but she can still fit into her wedding gown. I don't think she has aged much since we met."

"Jacob Lowen, my goodness, you're going to make me blush. Anyway, it's a miracle that I haven't aged twice as fast, married to you!"

Holly smiled at the loving exchange she was witnessing. "I hope when I do find Mr. Right that we'll have the kind of relationship I see you two have. This may be the best assignment I ever had. The fringe benefits of seeing how a good marriage works may make me want to pay the bureau for the privilege. At least let me buy supper."

"Thanks but ...."

Holly interrupted Jake, "Hey, it's your tax dollars at work, don't knock it. What looks good on the menu?"

After a relaxed meal where the conversation drifted between favorite restaurants and more about the Phoenix area. Holly asked the Lowens about their life in Chicago and if the transition was difficult.

"Leaving friends was hard for me, but I can breathe so much better here. Anyway, living here means that we will have visitors, especially during the Chicago winter." A cloud crossed Samantha face as she was thinking about the visit from Leila and Vinny that ended in tragedy.

Jake and Holly both noticed it and Jake leaned over and touched Samantha's arm.

"Without making it obvious, can we retrace your steps that night and see where Vinny was?"

"He was playing blackjack; we can show you the table. Then he drifted over toward the craps table where Cindy's....," at a loss for words, Jake stumbled on how to describe Harold and Cindy's relationship. "Boyfriend and potential future husband was winning big."

"Did you notice him before you saw him at the blackjack table?" asked Holly.

"No, I was losing my limit of $10 on the roulette wheel." admitted Samantha.

"Now that you mention it, I think I saw him come in as we were coming out from dinner, so he must not have been in the casino very long. He and Leila must have had dinner earlier somewhere else and he came here after. I wonder why Leila didn't come with him."

"That's easy Jake, she can't stand the lights and the noise, she gets a headache. She told me that when we were together at our house. You and Vinny were talking and she mentioned how Vinny wanted to go to the casinos but she refused to accompany him. It was one of the few things she ever stood up to him about. He didn't really care; he liked flirting with the cocktail waitresses. Leila thinks he was unfaithful to her more than once. She always insisted on being checked for STDs when she had a physical exam. Leila is not as dumb as she looks or rather as dumb as Vinny thought she was."

Holly looked puzzled. "If Vinny was such a creep, why did she stick with him? There were no kids to worry about, were there?"

"Leila is a devout Catholic; divorce was out of the question. She knew she married the wrong man, she as much as admitted it to me, but she couldn't divorce him, bum that he was."

"Wow, her life, if she recovers fully, will be different now." mused Holly.

"It certainly will be. I imagine that she will be quite well off, at least enough to live comfortably. I would not be surprised if she moved from Chicago, maybe to Florida. I think she has a sister living there. She will be a wealthy and not unattractive widow, but I don't think she'll fall for another Vinny type, at least I hope not."

"You still feel protective of her, don't you Sam?"

"Yes, I do, Jake. I can't help feeling this way toward her." admitted Samantha.

Holly proved a skilled blackjack player, parlaying her stack of $100 worth of chips into $250 before quitting.

"Great playing, if you ever decide to leave your current occupation, you could consider card sharking."

"Thanks Uncle Jake, but I know enough about the odds to avoid that. I did have a good run though. I will need to check with Herb about how to handle my winnings. I was using company money. Fortunately I didn't win enough to trigger a W-2G. Maybe I can lose it at the craps table and make my life simpler. One thing for sure, our friend didn't see anyone while he was playing blackjack, the lines of sight are wrong. So you were right in thinking that whoever he saw, he saw later."

Before drifting over to the craps table, Samantha tried her luck at the roulette wheel. This time she quit when she was ahead by $50 rather than push her luck. Jake indicated his pleasure at her restraint as gambling was not a habit he wanted Samantha to fall into.

Retracing their steps as much as possible from the roulette wheel to the where they were standing when they saw Vinny cross their path, the Lowens were surprised to see Cindy and Harold Rousseau at the table. Harold was rolling the dice. Touching Holly's arm, Jake indicated they should stop here for a while before moving to the table. Holly, recognizing Cindy, made a slight nod of her head in agreement. She took in the mirrors and understood how the Lowens felt that Vinny had seen someone, mostly likely in the mirror, who was at the table. From where they were standing, they had a good view of the players. Cindy looked up and apparently saw them as she gave a slight touch on Harold's arm. This was not at all visible from straight on as there was a crowd of people blocking the trio's direct view of the table. But watching in the mirror as they were, all three noticed the slight movement clearly. They saw Harold look up at the mirror and after another two passes of dice, hand them over to the dealer and collect his chips. He headed for the cashier's office while Cindy moved in their direction apparently to keep them from following Harold.

"What a surprise to see you here! Having any luck?"

"Hi Cindy. Holly had a little, I won my small stake at roulette and Jake as usual kept his money in his pocket."

"How did Harold do?" inquired Jake.

"Okay, he is a little ahead, but wanted to quit early."

Holly said lightly, "Great, I'd love to meet him. Where did he go?"

"He cashed out and went to get the car; he has a headache and wants to go home. Maybe another time. See you tomorrow for lunch, Holly," as Cindy headed for the door.

"He certainly seemed to want to avoid us, didn't he." mused Jake.

"I wonder what name he is using."

"I tried to find out, with no luck," admitted Jake.

"Yes, but you didn't have one of these, did you?" Holly opened her purse so that Sam and Jake could see her FBI badge. "Keep an eye on which cage he goes to, I want to follow him but not too closely. Here, hold on to my chips for a while."

Coming back from the cashier's booth, Holly reported to the Lowens. "Calls himself 'Goodwin, Charles Goodwin.' It took a while. The cashier had to call the floor manager who in turn called the house manager, but finally I got his name and social security number. I will have Tom run it tomorrow."

"Did you ask the guy if this Charles Goodwin is a regular?"

'The cashier sees so many players that he really doesn't pay attention to their faces, so he can't say. We will check the surveillance cameras; they have them covering all the booths so that the cashiers can't short the house and so if any player complains of being shorted, they can do an instant replay. Most casinos keep them for a few months. Didn't you say your friend; Deputy Lodestone had a relative working here. Can you give him a call, Jake while I call Tom?"

Within ten minutes, she was joined by Tom Roberts and another agent, John Marshall. After briefing them on what she had seen, Holly turned the investigation over to them, since she didn't want to blow her cover any more than she already had at the cashier window. Questioned about it later by Jake, she admitted that she had taken a chance but that she needed to find out what name Harold Rousseau was using to cash in his winnings. She reminded Jake how he had, by a stratagem, been able to discover that Harold wasn't using Rousseau at the casino.

Obtaining copies of the surveillance tapes, the FBI agents were able to get good photos of both Cindy Rousseau and the man the Lowens knew as Harold. The next morning, Tom rang the Lowens to report to Holly what they had found out. Tom was able to demand to see the records of winnings and from it learned that the casino had issued a half dozen form W-2Gs to Charles Goodwin. He was considered a regular whose winnings totaled around $50,000 over the last two months. While the casino did not keep track of the losses incurred by their patrons, an interrogation of dealers that evening indicated that several remembered the man calling himself Charles Goodwin who the dealers agreed was a high roller. Again, no one wanted to commit themselves to any amount but a couple of dealers, when pressed, admitted they had seen Goodwin drop $10,000 or more at their table before quitting. Shown the photos of Cindy, most didn't recognize her, but the ones who did, agreed that, when she was with Harold, she curbed his gambling. Tom was running a check on the social security number and any priors that Goodwin had and would get back to Holly.

Chapter Twenty One

Right on time, Cindy pulled in to collect Holly for lunch. They had speculated over breakfast if Cindy would back out of the lunch date and when she showed, Jake and Samantha were more than curious.

"What I wouldn't give to be a fly on the wall during that conversation."

"Samantha, whatever are you thinking? You know how most of these restaurants swat flies. What a terrible way to go. Anyway, you needn't bother, Holly is wearing a wire, Tom will be in a van nearby recording every word."

"Where was she hiding the microphone?"

"In the pin on her dress. The micro electronics they use now are so small and sensitive that the days of cumbersome microphones are long over."

"Did she take her badge and gun, Jake?"

"Of course, she is required to."

Jake puttered around his office the rest of the afternoon, ostensibly working on a new novel in which his hero, a veteran of the Civil War moved west. Questioned on this by Samantha, Jake admitted he was trying to branch out to encompass their new location. Further pressed by Samantha, Jake admitted that it would give him the excuse to drag her around western sites as well as allow Jake to acquire more books (background research) and more guns (adding color to the narrative). Fortunately Jake's novels sold well, better than his scholarly books, so Samantha was inclined to give in to both his expenditures and his schemes. But Jake found his thoughts far from 1870s and more to the present day as he realized that he was nervously awaiting the return of Holly.

Stopping in the kitchen for a cup of coffee, he commented to Sam. "It's almost like she is our real niece. I feel responsible for her."

"Probably because she is so close in age to our own children. By the way, I got an email from Heather. She and the kids want to come for a visit in August before the kids go back to school. I emailed back and told her it was okay."

"All our company should be gone by then. Will Don be able to come?"

"No, he is scheduled for a business meeting in Greece, though that could change. If it does, he will try to join them." Don was their son-in-law of whom Jake was particularly fond. He and Jake shared many interests and while Jake had been protective of Heather (overly protective according to Samantha); he was pleased with their daughter's choice of a husband. And the grandkids were great.

ust as Jake was getting ready to take Jasmine for a walk, Holly came in.

Both Lowens crowded around to get the news.

"Pretty much the same story she told you. She admitted that she isn't sure it's going to work with Harold. He was nice enough when he was married and they were having an affair, but now that the divorce is going through, she is beginning to have more sympathy for the ex-wife. It is all on tape; Tom will deliver a typescript later this afternoon."

"UPS again?"

"Fed Ex this time. But the real news is how she was pumping me for information on Leila."

"Pumping you?" puzzled Samantha.

"Thought I might have met her during one of my visits to you in Chicago. She started on the angle that I probably had met her, what a shame she was attacked, and then worked around to trying to find out if Leila had identified her assailant. She seemed to have more than a casual interest in what Leila knew. Also wanted to know about these personal therapists, why her brother-in-law was flying them in, wouldn't locals be cheaper?"

'Hmmm. She doesn't strike me as the naturally curious type. I took her to be more like an empty headed showgirl."

'Sorry to contradict you, Uncle Jake, but the airhead routine is only an act. Cindy is a shrewd and intelligent woman. It's my guess she figured out that Harold or Charles, whatever his name is, is good for a lot of dough and she intends to get a share of it. Any way she can."

"How did she react to Leila's staying here?" queried Samantha.

"Better than yesterday, she seems to have regained her composure. No more talk of crime statistics that frighten her. She is a strong person, but then a showgirl would need to be. Muscular, I wouldn't be surprised if she still works out. Maybe that is where she goes every day."

"Any more on Harold?"

"Not really, Jake. She repeated her story, as if to reinforce it in my mind, but I already said that. She didn't let on his real identity and of course I didn't say anything about my discovery after they left. If I were Harold, I'd watch my back. She might not have any scruples about getting her hands on as much money as she could and clearing out."

"Are you getting together again?"

95

"No plans, Samantha. Just the vague, we should do this again. I tried to drop a hint about wanting to find a place to work out, but she didn't volunteer to introduce me to her club."

"That is really strange because usually you get a discount yourself if you bring a new member."

"That's right, Samantha. It made me suspicious. I am going to ask Tom to have her followed and find out where she goes."

"If she is so smart, won't she spot a tail?"

"This is your tax dollars at work, Jake. When Tom drops off the manuscript he is also going to drop off a magnetic honing device. When we get the chance we will put one on the back bumper of Cindy's car. He already tagged Harold's car last night at the casino. Our guys can track them without being seen."

"Wow, I'm glad I'm law abiding."

"Speaking of being law abiding, how would the two of you like to join me at the police range tomorrow. I need to qualify and probably you haven't had the opportunity to practice since you moved out here. And you really should, since both of you have concealed carry permits."

"How did you know …?"

"Trade secrets, Samantha, trade secrets. What about it?"

Chapter Twenty Two

"Mind if I pack some Civil War era weapons with to use at the pistol range? They are a bear to clean but I need to verify some details on what actually is possible with a cap and ball revolver."

"No problem, Jake, we have reserved the range for whole morning for agency use. There are enough firing points for all the agents who need to qualify as well for you and Samantha. I wouldn't be surprised if some of the guys want to try their hand with your revolvers, I certainly would."

"Be my guest, niece, or don't we need to keep up the pretense there?"

"We don't, but it's better if we stay in character if you don't mind being called uncle?"

"I'm getting used to it. What calibers can we bring? I want to start competing in Cowboy Shooting and would love to try my shotgun on the silhouette targets."

"The range we're using is good for all handguns and the police also use it for shotgun practice. It's not certified for high power rifle or at least that is what Tom told me. I will need to qualify on that range at another time."

Joining them, Sam remarked, "How much stuff are you bringing, Jake?"

"Well, I have a Colt .44 Army, a Colt .36 Navy, a LeMat and a Spiller and Burr representing Confederate arms manufacturing. Then I'm taking a Colt in .45 Long Colt, and Remington copy in .357. Then, of course the Judge in .45/.410, your Ladysmith in .38 Special and the 9mm Glock. Oh, and my new double barrel coach gun in 12 gauge."

"Just don't ask me to help you clean them. You know how you complain about getting the black powder residue off."

"Maybe I can talk Holly into helping, or better yet, maybe Tom would like to come for dinner and get a lesson in cleaning black powder weapons."

Holly chuckled. "I'll be glad to help. Tom isn't allowed to come over except in disguise. I doubt if the neighbors would understand why the UPS truck in parked in your driveway for a couple of hours. It might make them dump their UPS stock."

The police range was on the other side of Phoenix. When they first got there, all three were firing the modern weapons. After she qualified with both of her duty weapons, Holly offered to let Samantha and Jake a turn.

"Samantha, you turned in quite a score with my .40 caliber on the silhouette target. Would you like to use it to shoot some of the combat course where the targets are more challenging?"

"Sure, Holly, I hate to admit it in front of Jake, but this is really fun. I actually like practicing with Jake's weapons."

The next set of targets involved multiple scenarios. As the targets presented themselves to the shooter, there was a split-second in which to decide whether to shoot. Some depicted criminals with guns pointing at you. Others were targets of policemen or civilians which if you shot at you lost points. The next level involved cutouts where the bad guy was standing behind a hostage and what was required was a careful head shot, if any shot was to be taken at all. When she saw these, Samantha gave an involuntary shudder.

"This was what the killer did when he was using Leila as a shield. I can see how this kind of training is useful."

Counting up their scores, Samantha was pleased to see that using Holly's duty pistol she had beat Jake's score by 10 points. Jake had been using a 9mm Glock from his collection.

"Great shooting, Sam. I'm glad to know you are defending our home. I can sleep more peacefully at night knowing you're on guard."

"Get real you big lunk."

"Seriously, I'm glad you can defend yourself. You did great this morning with everything you shot, including your own snub nose. I am proud of you. Do you want to join us for some black powder shooting?"

"I'll pass Jake; you know the blue smoke makes it hard for me to breathe. I wonder how asthmatics did in the Civil War."

"Probably didn't have to serve or if they couldn't get out of it, didn't last long. That would be an interesting research topic and might even make the plot of a novel. Asthmatic wants to serve the Union cause but can't because of his health and becomes a spy instead."

"Just be sure you give me credit in the acknowledgements for the idea, professor."

"You know I will Sam. After all aren't most of my books dedicated to you?"

"Do you mind if I try some of the Civil War weapons, Samantha? I'll join you in the clubhouse in a little while."

"Go ahead Holly. They're actually a lot of fun and it really helps to understand why paintings of Civil War battles always had a blue haze over the battle field."

Several of the special agents were interested in trying the weapons as well and Jake spent several minutes orienting them on to how to load and handle the percussion weapons.

Because barrel fouling is so common with black powder, Jake took particular care to demonstrate how to minimize fouling and how to be sure there was no obstruction in the barrel from a ball that hadn't cleared the barrel.

"Be sure to double check that you have charged the chamber with powder. If you seat a ball on an empty chamber it will lodge in the barrel and your next round will blow the gun up in your hand. In the heat of battle, there were many recorded instances of weapons exploding in the user's hand. We don't really know how common it was. Many who lost their revolver in this way probably also were killed by an enemy combatant." We have recovered revolvers from the battlefield that were not charged with powder so we know it was a common mistake in the heat of battle."

Content that his pupils were sufficiently impressed to be careful, Jake supervised the loading of the first two sets. He was more interested in the issue of accuracy and wanted to test his theories out on the targets. The agents were having so much fun that several of them volunteered to clean the revolvers with him at the club house after they were done. He got an invitation to come back and practice with them every month, with the proviso that he brought some of his antique collection with him.

'Jake is making quite an impression on the team, Samantha. He's a great instructor. I really enjoyed the history lesson and the chance to actually feel like I was part of history."

'Jake's a natural teacher, Holly. I know that he misses the classroom sometimes. But he hated grading. Oh, not the good students. Jake always felt he learned from them, but the ones who were only taking the course to get through. They weren't inspired, though Jake did manage to connect with some and make history come alive to them. He has had some of his undergrads go on and get advanced degrees; a couple of them credit Jake with turning them on to the field."

"Maybe while I am staying with you, Uncle Jake can practice his teaching style on me."

Samantha laughed. "Jake will lecture at the merest suggestion that someone is interested. Just ask him a couple of questions on some topic and sit back."

"I will. How much time do we have before Leila is discharged?"

"I got a call from Vitello this morning and then a few minutes later from the hospital. She is scheduled for discharge tomorrow. The trailer is being delivered this afternoon and Vitello's men will start living there when she is released."

"That's quicker than I expected, but I think we are ready. Glad we scheduled this for today."

Jake, Samantha and Holly pulled in to their driveway just as Cindy was leaving their front door.

"Hi, I left a note on the door, Harold and I are going to the Grand Canyon for a few days and I wanted to ask you to watch the house."

"We'll be glad to. Have a nice time," said Samantha.

After they had gone inside, Holly asked, "I thought you said he was lying low? I wonder why they are taking a trip. It must be hard either using cash all the time with so many motels insisting on having a credit card on file. Credit card usage can be traced. I wonder if they aren't worried about Harold's ex anymore."

"Maybe or maybe he just got cabin fever and needed to get out. Of course we only have her word that they are going to the Grand Canyon. Who knows where they are really headed." added Jake.

"You're forgetting our little bug; we managed to get them on both their cars. Hers while it was in the driveway and his at the casino last night. Actually, Tom tagged Harold's, credit where credit is due. He was following them at a safe distance and made his plates. Finding it in the parking lot was easy, especially since Harold used valet service."

Right on time the crew arrived with the Airstream. The Lowen's driveway had a level spot for RV parking off to one side of the garage and that is where Jake directed the trailer be placed. The previous owners had thoughtfully put a power hookup and a water tap in the right place so there was both. Emptying the holding tank would be trickier but the rental place had a contract to come out and empty the tank every couple of days.

Early in the evening, Tony LaMotte, the leader of Vitello's team stopped by the Lowens to check on arrangements. He made a list of what the team would still need. Jake learned from Tony there would be three others on the team, at least until they saw how things were going. Asked if the guys were bored with their duty, standing watch over Leila's hospital room, Tony answered that his team were professionals and had been selected for their abilities on the job and their ability to stay out of trouble off the job. Tony and one of the other guys were avaricious readers. The assignment provided ample time to indulge in that pastime. Looking over Jake's library, he asked if he could borrow a book or two while he was in residence.

"What is your main interest, Tony?"

"I am actually working on a degree from the University of Phoenix. I'll soon be done with my BA and am thinking about graduate study."

"That's great! What area?"

"Well, I really like science, but my job with Mr. Espennelli means that I can't really enroll in a regular program. However, I'm thinking about doing a study on the history of science since history is my second love."

Noticing the Civil War revolvers which Jake had been wiping down before putting them away, he asked if he could handle them. Jake took great pleasure in showing Tony how they were loaded and described his experiments in accuracy without letting on that the experiments were conducted at the police range.

"If you could find the time to go out with me, I would love that. I am familiar with modern weapons, but these historical arms fascinate me. It must be great to teach about them."

"There is nothing I like better, Tony, than to teach. Once we get into a routine with Leila and the nurses, we can go to a local range with the guns. Would any of your colleagues like to go as well?"

"I think you figured out that all of us are bodyguards, so we're all trained in using firearms as well as unarmed combat. Probably all the guys would like to go. I know Larry, he's the other big reader, is a history buff. He is always reading about battles and stuff. Do you have any Revolutionary war guns?"

"A couple. I have a flintlock pistol and a Brown Bess musket that I used in class to demonstrate what it would be like on a revolutionary war battlefield. Hold on a second, I'll get it from my gun safe."

While Jake was gone, Tony looked around the office. The photographs made from the casino video tapes caught his eye and he picked them up to examine them closely. He was still looking at them when Jake returned.

"Sorry, I shouldn't have been poking around your desk, but I thought I recognized the person in this photo."

"Who do you think it is, Tony?"

"Just some guy from Chicago. Couldn't be him, though. Does this guy live around here?"

"Actually, he lives next door. Calls himself Harry Rousseau but that's not his real name."

"How well do you know him, Dr. Lowen?"

"Not well at all. He and his companion keep to themselves. Holly, my niece, had lunch with Cindy Rousseau yesterday. She could tell you more."

"Thanks, now how does this musket work?"

Chapter Twenty Three

After Tony left, Jake asked Samantha if Holly was still up. When he learned she had gone to bed, pleading fatigue, Jake insisted she wake her up. In ten minutes, the women joined Jake in the kitchen where he had heated water for tea.

"Join me in a cup of herbal tea, Holly?"

"Jake, I don't know how you can drink that stuff. It has no taste."

"Samantha, for all your wonderful traits, learning to drink herbal tea is not one of them, i soothes the soul and calms your nerves. I find it a great aid to help me sleep."

"Jake in the thirty-five years I have been married to you, you have never had trouble sleeping, herbal tea or no herbal tea."

Throughout this exchange, Holly sat silent but smiling.

Jake wondered what she was thinking and was tempted to ask her but instead announced, "I have mint tea, sweet orange, raspberry…why don't you just help yourself from this drawer."

"Thanks, Uncle Jake. I assume you didn't wake me up to let me enjoy the wonderful exchange between you and Aunt Samantha. I hope I don't offend you, but I really think you two have a wonderful relationship. I am so thankful for the opportunity to live here. And see a great example of how a married couple should be. I'll bet your kids tell you that all the time."

"Thank you, Holly. Actually our children do tell us that, but I can't see how we did that much right."

"As usual, you're being too modest Samantha, but that is one of the things I love about you. Holly, I asked Samantha to wake you because I need to tell you about my conversation with Tony LaMotte the head of Vitello Espennelli's security team. I brought Tony into my study where we could sit and talk. He noticed the revolvers we used this morning and one thing led to another. When I left the room to retrieve a musket from the gun safe, he saw the photos of the neighbors on my desk. He was studying the one of Harold Rousseau when I returned. When I asked him about it, he said he thought it was a guy from Chicago, but was probably mistaken. I think he recognized Rousseau but didn't want to identify him to me."

"Interesting, Jake. Do you think Rousseau is someone connected to the mob?"

"I think so, Holly. I wouldn't be surprised if Vitello is getting another late night call from Phoenix as we speak. Only this time, no matter who Vitello is with, he's taking the call."

Samantha asked, "Do you think the Rousseaus are in danger? I would hate for something to happen to Cindy because she was in the clutches of Harold."

"Sam, I share your distaste for Harold, but Cindy is a big girl and should know what she is doing."

"It's too late to call either Herb or Tom; I'll touch base with them first thing in the morning. Again, good work, Jake. Goodnight again to both of you."

That postponed call was something Holly would later come to regret.

Chapter Twenty Four

"Jake, wake up! Jasmine is growling."

"What …oh I had incorporated her growling into my dream. I was working on another plot. What time is it?"

"Two AM. Jake, that is not like Jasmine. Something's up. Check it out, will you?"

"Give me a second to get fully awake and put on a pair of pants."

Grabbing his revolver, the Judge, loaded with two chambers of .410 shot and three of .45 ACP, Jake snatched a flashlight and headed for the living room. In the hallway, he bumped into someone. Pointing the light at the other person, he was relieved to see it was Holly carrying her duty pistol.

"I heard Jasmine and became suspicious. Sorry if I scared you, Jake."

"It's okay; I forgot you were staying here. My pulse rate is going back to normal. I'm glad I didn't shoot you or you me."

"Is someone in the house?" asked Holly, her voice a register above a whisper.

"No, Jasmine would bark and carry on a ruckus if we had an intruder. The sound she made is the 'something's outside that doesn't belong there' growl."

Jake and Holly found the dog in the kitchen, looking toward the Rousseau's house.

"Someone's prowling around the house next door. Cindy said they were leaving for the Grand Canyon so no one should be home, in spite of the car in the driveway. They must have taken Harold's car from the garage and left her car in the driveway to make it look like someone was home. Holly, check and see if there is a car out front."

In a few moments, Holly returned.

"I checked up and down the street. The prowlers did not come by car, or if they did, the driver has moved it out of sight. Should I call Tom or do we just want to alert the locals?"

"I'll call 911; you call Tom. I am going to request the responding units not use their lights and to block off the street if they have the manpower."

As Jake was putting down the phone from calling the sheriff, Jasmine emitted a low growl.

"Someone is coming out the back. Cover me, Holly."

Jake opened the sliding door and stepped out on the deck. Jasmine bolted past him and headed next door before he could get a hand on her collar.

We are committed now, thought Jake as he ran after the dog. I hope the sheriff's office responds quickly.

"Flashing his light on the shadowy figure, Jake yelled, "Stop or I'll shoot."

The only reply was a shot fired in his direction which caused him to duck behind the deck furniture. This won't stop a bullet. Why am I doing this pondered Jake. The squeal of tires indicated that the prowler had reached his getaway car. Holly joined him on the deck as did Samantha.

It was Samantha who spoke first. "What's going on? Are you playing hero again, Jacob Lowen? I won't ever speak to you again if you get yourself killed!"

"Relax, Samantha, the prowler next door took a shot at me, but either he was a really bad shot or he purposely missed me. I saw the muzzle flash and it was not aimed at me at all. Of course, he could've been nervous, but my intuition tells me otherwise."

"I didn't see the shot, Samantha. But the prowler had plenty of time to fire more than one round at Jake, but didn't."

The door bell interrupted their deliberations. Tom and Deputy Lodestone were at the front door.

Jake quickly filled them in on what they saw while Holly got dressed so she could accompany them next door. It was only then Jake realized Jasmine hadn't returned.

"Jasmine, Jasmine, where are you, girl?"

He was rewarded by hearing a lively barking, coming from the Rousseaus. Waiting for Tom and Lodestone to join him, Jake led them to the garage where they found Jasmine.

"That's really strange. The dog is untouched; they just trapped her in the garage. He had a gun, why not just shoot her?" asked Lodestone.

"That fits in with the shot fired way over my head. These are strange burglars. Since we are investigating a burglary, do we need a search warrant to enter the premises?" asked Jake.

"We don't know if the house is really empty, there could be someone injured inside. We have the obligation to enter and search for victims. Let me check in with my other units."

Lodestone called the other cars responding to the 911 call. The prowlers had made their getaway in a dark sedan; the closest car lost it when it got on the 101. Going next door,

105

they found that entry had been made through the back door by the garage. Whatever they were looking for, it was not your regular burglary. Nothing of value was taken. Druggies usually steal things they can easily pawn, but nothing appeared to be disturbed.

Since the ground was damp with dew and the prowlers had come across the lawn, their footprints were clearly visible on the light colored carpet. Jake made a mental note to tell Samantha on how wise her choice of tile and hardwood flooring was. Jake was no expert but it appeared there were two assailants and they were checking each room as a pair. His amateur detecting was confirmed by Lodestone.

"From these tracks, they were going room by room, looking for occupants. It remains me of how we were trained in the Marines to check out a house. These footprints bring to mind professionals. It looks like a hit team to me. Samantha or Holly, did you hear the shot fired at Jake?"

"I was inside on the phone, but no, I don't think I heard a shot."

"Come to think of it, I saw him aim at me and saw a muzzle flash, but I didn't hear a report. At the time I put it down to the theory that you never hear the one that kills you, but now I'm not sure."

"There was a shot fired at you or rather in your direction to keep you down, we just found a 9 mm casing by the garage back door. I think the guy who fired was using a silenced weapon." volunteered Tom.

"I've heard about acrimonious divorces, but hiring a hit team probably sets some kind of new low," declared Jake.

"Actually, Jake, it's more common than you think. The FBI has investigated a number of cases where the wife or husband hired someone to kill their former or soon to be former spouse. Of course, many just try to kill the spouse themselves. Maybe you remember the Drew Peterson case in Chicago? They suspect him of killing both his third and fourth wives when they wanted out of the marriage."

"I do remember the case in Chicago, Tom. Did you have anything to do with the investigation?"

"Not personally, but the Bureau was involved. Deputy Lodestone, can you have your crime scene team go over the house?"

"Certainly, Agent Roberts. We want to get to the bottom of this."

Later over coffee, decaf all around, Tom, Holly, Jake and Sam talked over the incident. With Jasmine contentedly resting at Jake's feet, Jake repeated how strange he found their treatment of Jasmine.

You're there to commit a murder, probably a double murder, yet you merely lock up the ,og. I don't get it."

Neither do I, Jake." replied Holly. "It was almost, almost like she knew the prowlers.)id you notice she stopped barking when she got to the house?"

I didn't think of it at the time, but now I recall wondering what happened to her. The vhole thing unfolded so fast, it's only now that the anomalies are starting to hit me."

;amantha spoke up, "Did you tell Tom about Tony LaMotte's apparent identification of he man who calls himself Harold Rousseau?"

'Tom, I'm sorry, I was going to call you in the morning. When Tony, Vitello's lead guy, vas in Jake's office, he saw the photo of the man next door made from the surveillance apes. Jake thinks he recognized the man."

'Do you think his recognition and the attempted hit tonight are connected, Jake?"

'I don't know. Tony certainly downplayed any recognition, but I did mention it was the ;uy next door."

'That's enough for me. I am getting a warrant to search the place. I'll have the sheriff's ifffice post a guard around the house. Harold Rousseau, Charles Goodwin or whoever he s will get the full Bureau treatment."

'Speaking about full Bureau treatment, how is the homing device on Harold's car doing, ['om?" asked Holly.

'It's parked at a long term parking lot near Sky Harbor airport. Not airport parking, one if those off site lots. If you are looking to lose a car, that isn't the way to do it. It's a way o lose a tail. Our guys were hanging back to avoid being spotted. The vehicle stopped ince for about five minutes. Retracing their route, the team realized it was in front of a otel where there's a Hertz rental counter. My guess is they prearranged a rental which vas waiting for them at the hotel. Either Harold dropped off Cindy and their bags or she lropped him off and then left the car at the off-site parking. Whoever left it, hopped a ;huttle to the airport where the other one was waiting with the rental. I'm going to get he boys to go over the car for prints and anything else they can find. Like traces of lime hat we found in the trunk of Willie Carlinski's abandoned automobile."

'Can you arrange an interception of their mail, Tom?" asked Jake.

'Not unless we have reason to suspect a crime is being committed through the mail, vhy?"

"Because I think they're only hanging around because they need to collect their new identities. They didn't want to take a chance, post 911, on counterfeit passports and are waiting for new ones to come in their new names." volunteered Jake.

"More coffee or sweet rolls, anyone?" asked Samantha, adding, "I don't think we are going to see Harold and Cindy around anymore. Somehow they will collect their passports and clear out."

"What makes you say that, Samantha?" asked Tom.

Before Samantha could answer, Jake broke in. "Woman's intuition and let me tell you after thirty-five years, Sam is seldom wrong. She is able to sense what is going to happen."

"That's a handy trait, Samantha. Would you like to work for the FBI?" inquired Tom.

"Thanks, but I can't turn it on. I just get an impression that I can't shake and it's nearly always correct."

"That's how she came to marry me," joked Jake, "I made an impression on her she couldn't shake!" He ducked as Samantha took a swing at him.

"I'll make an impression on you, you teller of tall tales!"

"Sam, remember, you're threatening to assault me in the presence of two law enforcement officers."

"No jury of my peers would ever convict me; they would give me a medal for what I put up with, Jacob Lowen."

Holly and Tom watched with amusement as the obviously loving couple enacted their pantomime. Holly whispered to Tom, "I think that this playful interaction is part of the secret of their happy marriage. That and the fact that Samantha is a damn good shot and Jake knows it."

Chapter Twenty Five

Nobody got much sleep the rest of the night. Jake dozed a bit in his recliner, Holly and Samantha kept each other company in the kitchen, the adrenaline rush giving them a desire to bake. Only Jasmine, the canine security alarm, was able to sleep. Curled up in a ball next to Jake's recliner, she slept contently as if nothing had disturbed her night's rest. She actually dropped off before Tom Roberts left, causing the quartet to wonder if the hit men had slipped her a tranquilizer laced treat. Jake told Samantha if Jasmine was acting strange in any way in the morning, he would take her to the vet. Jake had found a vet for Jasmine before he had found a physician for himself. At the time, Samantha commented that he took better care of the dog than he did of himself. Jake defended his actions by pointing out that Jasmine couldn't drive herself to a vet, thus he needed to care for her and furthermore she was a great watch dog.

The events of the night or rather the early morning had proven Jake right. With the Rousseaus gone, there was no telling when the break-in would have been detected. As Tom Roberts said as he was leaving, Jasmine's warning might have greater consequences than any of them, including the dog, could imagine. The FBI crime scene team was on its way and would be giving the house a thorough going over.

Finally, with the aroma of fresh baked bread, sweet rolls and a chocolate fudge cake filling the kitchen and wafting into the rest of the house, Samantha and Holly called it a morning and caught a couple hours of sleep.

At nine AM, Jake gently shook Sam awake.

"The hospital just called. They're loading Leila in the ambulance and she should be here in about a half hour."

"Oh… I just have time for a quick shower. I'm so glad that rental place was able to move the hospital bed in the other day. I think everything is ready."

Thirty-three minutes later the procession arrived. First came the ambulance, then two dark colored full size sedans, followed by a chartreuse colored compact car. Out of the last car, a middle aged woman in a nursing uniform came at a brisk walk to the rear doors of the ambulance as the EMTs were bringing out the gurney with Leila. The two sedans disgorged Tony and three other muscular men, who in typical body guard mode, scanned the street and homes that lined it. Jake wondered if it was his imagination but he thought he detected the outlines of shoulder holsters under their jackets. Two of the men stayed outside, while Tony and another man accompanied the gurney into the house. Jake had put Jasmine in his study to keep her out of the way and curb her enthusiastic reception of their guests. Jake and Samantha had discussed stratagems for keeping Jasmine contained in their part of the house and out of Leila's room.

Getting Leila settled took the better part of an hour, even after the ambulance left. She was still on an IV drip and the nurse made sure everything was set up correctly. Tony and his men settled into the trailer and parked their vehicles with the front of the vehicles facing the street for a quick departure if needed. The driveway was constructed so both of Tony's cars could be lined up nose to tail, allowing Jake and Samantha access to their vehicles. The extra parking spaces and deeper than normal garage were selling points for Jake who hoped to recommence his car collecting hobby.

Around 10:30 the nurse came out. "She seems to be doing fine, her vitals are stable."

"Can I see her?" asked Samantha.

"You can look in, but she's sleeping now. I'll get you when she wakes up."

After the nurse disappeared back into Leila's room, Holly asked Tony where and his men were going to keep watch.

"In Leila's room, round the clock," he replied and left to get his men settled.

"What will they do all day?" asked Holly.

"They aren't there for medical care, they will probably read." Replied Samantha.

"Or listen to their I-Pods," joked Holly.

"They may read, but they won't listen to music. Their job is twofold. One to protect Leila from any possible attack and the other to listen to anything she might say, even in her sleep which will lead Vitello to Vinny's killer." corrected Jake.

"So she might have recognized the person who killed her husband?"

"Yes, Holly, that's Vitello's theory. Vinny saw someone who he shouldn't have seen and that person or another unknown person killed him for it. Judging from where her body was found, she was being used as a shield as she was marched toward the room where Vinny was hiding."

"Vitello would like to avenge Vinny, no matter who killed him. He wouldn't hesitate to order a hit, would he?" asked Holly.

"Are you connecting the dots as well?" responded Jake.

"It's possible the attack next door and Vinny's murder are connected," replied Holly.

"Maybe, just maybe you're right, which means ……" Jake was interrupted by a knock on the door. Tony came in from the trailer.

110

I just wanted to be sure everything is okay, Dr. and Mrs. Lowen. Oh, I'm sorry. I didn't now you had a guest."

Come in and meet Samantha's niece, Holly Tan. Holly is from back East and will be taying with us for a while."

Pleased to meet you Ms. Tan, Tony LaMotte. Perhaps the Lowens have explained our ather interesting housing arrangements?"

'Pleased to meet you, Mr. LaMotte. Yes, they have. But I think things will work out, ·ven though to Samantha it's like Grand Central Station."

'If it wouldn't be considered too casual, I would prefer if you call me Tony."

'Okay, Tony, please call me Holly."

'Dr. Lowen, what's with the Smokeys next door and the crime scene tape?"

'Seems there was a break-in last night. My dog alerted us and we called 911."

'Gee! I thought this was a safe area. That was one of the reasons Mr. Espennelli wanted ais sister-in-law to recover here. Any one injured or was it just a robbery?"

'The people who live there weren't home. We don't know what, if anything was stolen." eplied Jake.

'Out for the evening or on vacation?" queried Tony.

'Not sure how long they'll be gone. They asked us to keep an eye on the house while hey were away. Guess Jasmine overheard that conversation."

Samantha asked, "Do you have everything you need out there? Is there anything I can get you?"

'No, we're well catered for. One of the guys picked up everything we need at Wal-Mart. We'll be doing a lot of our own cooking, at least the guys on duty. When we are off juty, we hit the local restaurants. Over the last few weeks we have become quite familiar with the restaurants in the area."

'I would love to hear your recommendations, Tony," chimed in Holly.

"Ms. Tan, er Holly, I'd be honored if you'd let me take you to some of my favorites, unless you have an attachment that you are not advertising on your left hand."

Laughing, Holly replied. "No attachments. In fact, I'm in the process of shedding an unfortunate relationship. But does your work schedule permit hosting women to eating establishments?"

"Well, Mr. Espennelli is very particular about how we conduct ourselves on assignment. He doesn't approve of us dating or even clubbing around while on duty. That's why we're housed in accommodations with all the amenities of home. We've arranged for cable access in the trailer as well as high speed internet. But we aren't allowed to entertain guests."

"How constraining. If that's the case, why are you asking me out to dinner?"

"Well, it isn't exactly a date. After all I have to eat and though you are an attractive woman, we are, for all intents and purposes, living under the same roof, I think the boss would understand."

"Sort of checking out the house guests for security clearance?"

Blushing, Tony responded to Holly's jibe. "Not really, but I guess it looks like that, doesn't it?"

"Sort of, but it's okay. I'd be glad to go to dinner with you."

"How about tonight, say 5:30?"

"Okay."

"Tony, before you go, Holly and I did some baking this morning, would you and your crew like to take this chocolate cake?"

"Thank you, Mrs. Lowen. Thank you very much."

Samantha handed over the cake, ignoring the pained look on Jake's face as he saw his favorite cake head out the door.

"Well, Tony is certainly a fast mover."

"He certainly is, Holly." agreed Samantha.

Jake, still looking pained over the departure of the cake, managed to rejoin the conversation. "Do you think he's trying to pump you for information, Holly?"

"Probably, but I doubt he's been through the FBI course on getting information from suspects. Just by what he asks will tell me a lot."

"Do you two think he had something to do with the break-in?"

I wouldn't be surprised, Sam. Too many coincidences for me. He happens to see the hoto on my desk and the house next door is hit"

Why not wait until they moved in, Jake?" asked Samantha.

Because he couldn't control when Leila was being discharged, but it is interesting that he break-in occurred before they moved in. Their trailer would have been between our ouse and the Rousseaus. Last night was the only time to keep them from being involved. They couldn't help being witnesses to any break-in and be questioned as to what they aw and heard. Another thing, if Tony recognized Harold, Harold might recognize Tony nd maybe others on his crew once they moved in to guard Leila. He might have gotten the wind up and fled. No, they needed to move fast, but didn't expect them to be gone." offered Holly.

'I think you are right, Holly, Tony is fairly high up in Vitello's organization. He would ecognize any key people. That probably one of the reasons Vitello put him in charge of his operation."

'Jake, do you think it was Harold Rousseau or at least the guy we are calling Harold that Tony recognized?" asked Samantha.

'I think so, but the question is what's his real name. Holly, has the Bureau come up with anything on Charles Goodwin?"

'Tom called earlier, Charles Goodwin is looking very good for a person who's been dead for fifteen years. The social security number is correct, but the Charles Goodwin who was issued that number is dead. Either the wrong person was buried in Goodwin's grave or someone stole his identity."

Samantha sighed. "This whole mystery seems to revolve around people who are using other identities. What's the chance that the person buried in Goodwin's grave isn't Goodwin?"

'That's what Tom is tracking down. It's possible that Goodwin wanted to do a bunk and either because of an accident of identification or a purposeful deception, he had the opportunity."

'But what about the story of the ex-wife wanting Harold's money?" asked Jake.

'Could be true. Let's say for the sake of argument, Harold is really Charles Goodwin and he didn't die fifteen years ago. Let's say he creates the identity he is fleeing from. To make things easier, let's call his created identity, Harold Smith. He marries. The marriage goes sour. He has his old identity to fall back on, maybe he's even stashed some money away in that name. He doesn't want to share this with his wife and takes off, but because Charles is considered dead and because it has been useful to have this name, he decides to create another identity just as he created Harold Smith or whatever his name was."

"Whee, I'm glad you're working for the good guys, Holly. You have the makings of a good criminal mind."

"Thanks, Samantha. I think that was a compliment."

"Or the making of a fine novelist and that is a compliment. I really like that story line, mind if I use it in a novel? You might actually get me to break into the 20th century if not the 21st with a plot like that. Of course, I'll give you credit in the acknowledgements."

Laughing, Holly said, "Great Jake, I'll look forward to reading it. Do you mind if I borrow your car, Samantha? I need to run down town to the office."

"Of course, Holly."

"If anyone asks, I'm out shopping."

Chapter Twenty Six

ake retired to his study where, in spite of his fatigue, he was able to put in several good hours of writing. Samantha sat with Leila for a two prolonged periods, holding her hand and seemingly bringing comfort to her friend. The nurse took the opportunity to slip outside, but one of Tony's crew, Orlando, sat quietly in the corner. At first it unnerved Samantha, but she grew used to his silent presence. It wasn't a brooding or heavy presence, more like a relative or friend watching in a sick room while you visited with a sleeping or unconscious person. Samantha wondered what it would be like when Leila was fully awake. Would she resent the intrusion of her privacy or accept it for what it was meant to be, protection against her being harmed again? A couple of times, Leila tried to speak, but found the effort too great. She seemed content to occasionally look into Samantha's eyes. For her part, Samantha sensed that Leila had a peace about her she hadn't had all the time she was in the hospital. In spite of the disruption to their routine, Samantha felt she and Jake had made the right choice in opening their home.

Sitting there, Samantha wondered about the events of last night and how they might be connected to what had happened to Leila. It would be ironic if the person or persons who did this to Leila were living right next door. But that couldn't be. Neither Harold nor Cindy looked like what Samantha thought killers should look like. But Jake was always telling her the really good spies were those who didn't look like spies at all. She wondered if the same was true for murderers. Samantha gave an involuntary shudder. Their kids would reprimand her and Jake if they knew what they were into. After all the lectures she had given their children on choosing their friends carefully, here she had the widow of a mobster recovering from a murderous attack living in her house. Vitello was a mobster himself and four of his men were camped out in their driveway with access to the house. To compound all of that was the incident last night when apparently someone tried to kill their neighbors plus the added worry it might be someone at least contacted by Tony if it wasn't Tony himself.

Then there was Holly. Even though she wasn't really her niece, Samantha was starting to feel very protective of her. Could she really handle herself when she was out with Tony? What if he slipped something in her drink? Jake would think I'm crazy worrying like this but I can't help it. It's like we're caught in a whirlpool and can't escape the current sucking us in and down.

For a moment, she regretted having moved away from their home and friends in Illinois. Maybe we should've stayed there. But Samantha recalled how difficult her asthma attacks had become and how much better she was, even just in the last two months. Jake seemed so much more relaxed since the move. Samantha realized how tired he'd become of teaching or rather the processes that went along with teaching, the grading and the tedious committee assignments. He had come home complaining about how the administration was squeezing every last drop of blood out the full time professors and hiring a raft of adjuncts to avoid adding cost. Even his dean, with whom he was on good terms, seemed relieved when Jake asked for early retirement knowing he could afford to hire two younger assistant professors for Jake's salary as a tenured full professor. Jake was more and more like his old self. Talking about ideas for projects, doing research, and churning out his very successful novels. And of course, buying books. Ones he needed to research his latest interest. But since his latest interest usually translated into a book deal or two that was also okay.

Samantha was snapped out her train of thought by Orlando's standing beside the hospital bed asking her if she could understand what Leila was trying to say. Straining to understand her friend, she finally made out Leila asking 'where's Vinny?'

The realization struck her like a proverbial ton of bricks; Leila didn't know Vinny was dead. Did she remember anything of the attack, or was the whole event erased from her memory? Puzzled by what to say to Leila about Vinny, Samantha decided she needed to tell her the truth.

"Leila, there was an …" Samantha paused, should she say accident? How should she describe what happened. But it suddenly become clear to her, in one of those moments of insight that Jake teased her about but which she knew instinctively was right. "Vinny was shot, Leila, at the same time you were shot."

"Is he dead?" Leila asked in a weak voice.

Without hesitation, Samantha said, "Yes, I'm so sorry, Leila."

As Leila's head dropped back on the pillow, Samantha thought she heard Leila whisper, "It's alright."

The nurse suggested perhaps Leila should be left alone to sleep and Samantha decided she had to do something about getting Jake some dinner. She had declined Vittelo's offer of a cook though she had accepted a cleaning service. For a moment she wondered if they should go out, but didn't feel comfortable about leaving her house full of strangers just yet.

Coming into the kitchen, she found Jake helping himself to a sweet roll.

"Hi, honey. I got a little peckish and needed some nourishment."

Resisting the temptation to reprimand Jake for spoiling his supper, Samantha merely asked, "Is Holly back yet?"

"No but she called on my cell phone 30 or 40 minutes ago. She wanted to report on the investigation next door. It doesn't appear that the Rousseaus were clearing out for good. They left some luggage, some of which was packed for colder weather."

Jake continued. "Since it's unknown how much they had in the way of clothes or luggage, they can't determine how much they took with them. One thing, there was no money left in the house. If Cindy is paying for everything with cash, she didn't leave any

116

of it there. Another thing was strange. The man's clothing they found was in two different sizes. Two vastly different sizes. Like pants that were size 44 and others that were size 34."

"So they might have left for good and just abandoned what they couldn't carry, especially if Harold had put on that much weight."

"Maybe Sam, maybe. But there were more in size 44 than in 34. Had Harold lost weight recently?"

"Not that I noticed, but we hardly saw him, only running into him at the casino."

"We just have to wait til they turn up. Want to hear how they managed the car switch?"

'Of course, do I have to ask you to tell me?"

'Thought you'd never ask. Pretty clever, need to use it in a book some time. Wonder if it would work with horses instead of cars?"

"Jacob Lowen you can try the patience of Job. Wait, don't say it, you're related to Job because you are both Mediterranean."

"Well, we are. Don't go acting like Job's wife on me. But since you insist, I'll tell you how they pulled it off. Three days before, Cindy reserves a car at Hertz. The day before they leave, she goes in and picks it up. Apparently moves from the Hertz spaces to another parking space in the hotel garage. Safe place to leave a car overnight, which is, after all, what hotel guests do. Next day she drops Harold off at the rental car with the luggage and takes off for the airport. It's not clear if she dropped him at the front door or by the garage. The hotel is fairly busy and no one notice a man being dropped off, even by a gorgeous blond."

Samantha treated Jake to one of her glares.

Jake ignored the glare and continued. "She might have had a scarf covering her hair. Anyway, she takes off and drops his car at the offsite long term parking, hops the shuttle back to the terminal. Has luggage with her, acts like she has a flight to catch. Makes a point of being seen, asks questions about retrieving her car, engages the shuttle driver in conversation, in short acting very unlike a modern air traveler who tries to make herself inconspicuous in those situations. It was easy for the driver and the attendants to remember her."

"Like she was trying to draw attention to herself."

"Right, if she wanted to slip away, she would have used airport long-term parking and avoided contact. And before you give me another of your glares, you've got to admit that

117

she is a good looking woman and not one that would be easily forgotten if she engaged you in conversation. Well, maybe not you, but most men would find her hard to forget."

"Jacob Lowen…"

Before she could continue, Jake interrupted. "Do you want to hear this story or not? If you are going to keep interjecting comments and treating me to those stares of yours. Anyway, where was I? Oh, yeah. So she gets dropped at the terminal, claims she is flying United, that was part of her patter with the shuttle driver, and disappears through the doors."

"Let me guess. No record of either her or Harold on United."

"Right, Sam. And no record of her on any other airlines. Of course it is possible she is flying under an alias using a different ID, but at least at the United counter no one recognized her photo. There are too many blondes flying out of Phoenix to totally eliminate the possibility except that there's no record of her on the security cameras inside the terminal. It appears she went in and then back out another door and got into the rental car which was driven by Harold. The rental car has an APB out on it, but with a 24 hour head start, they could be anywhere. L.A., even Denver, if they drove through the night. They could be across the border in Mexico."

"The Grand Canyon?"

"First place they checked, no car with those plates in the area."

"Do you think their new passports came and they took off?"

"That's why I mentioned L.A. and Denver. Those are the other two hubs though I guess they could have also reached Salt Lake City."

"Did you give your suggestions to Holly."

"I did, Sam, they're checking them out. Speaking about checking things out, what's for supper?"

Chapter Twenty Seven

Holly arrived back as Samantha was preparing supper. She was carrying a couple of shopping bags from stores in the Biltmore Fashion Park.

"Hi, smells good. Wish I could join you."

"Hi, Holly, looks like you've been busy. Get anything really nice?"

"Needed to bring something home as part of my cover story where I spent the afternoon. But yes, I did find some great stuff. Look at this little number."

Glancing at the little black dress Holly was holding up, Samantha hoped she wouldn't wear that around Jake. But she said, "Going to wear that tonight with Tony?"

Laughing heartily, Holly replied, "I'm not trying to seduce him, only get some information. No, I'm dressing a lot more conservatively tonight. I just couldn't resist it, and every woman needs one of these for when she is trying to attract male attention."

"No doubt about that dress on you attracting attention, but as your aunt, I'm glad you're not wearing it tonight."

"Wearing what tonight?" asked Jake as he ambled into the kitchen.

"Nothing, sweetheart. What else did you get, Holly?"

"Well, I got these shoes and this bag to match."

Clearing his throat, Jake intruded on the magic of the moment. "What's happening tonight?"

"Tom will be trailing me, at a discreet distance. We discussed my wearing a wire but didn't want to take a chance that Tony would tumble on to the surveillance van. Tom will be escorting another woman agent. I'm going to play it by ear. He might be trying to get information on the break-in or …"

"Or he might be interested in you as an attractive woman," volunteered Jake.

"We are thrown together or at least that's what he thinks. After all, I'm just your niece from back East. Has Leila said anything?"

Samantha related to Jake and Holly what happened in Leila's room and how she had told Leila that Vinny was dead. Leila seemed relieved at the news and Samantha thought a sense of peace had descended over her.

"Wasn't she happy in her marriage?" asked Holly.

"No, she wasn't happy, but wouldn't consider divorce. I think we were right. The real reason for the body guards is to find out if she can identify Vinny's killer. Vitello wants to handle avenging Vinny's death his way."

"Any more news on the whereabouts of the Rousseaus?"

"Nothing as yet. We have expanded the APB requesting any officer seeing the car not approach the suspects but keep it under surveillance and report to the local FBI office. We really don't have anything to arrest them on. It is not a crime to be the target of hit men, but we would want to take them into protective custody."

"Have fun on your date, Holly."

"Thanks, Jake."

When Holly left the kitchen, Jake and Samantha continued their conversation. Jake asked how Samantha felt about Leila.

"I'm happy for her. It was probably the only way out of the marriage for Leila and honestly, Vinny was a jerk."

"Just what I have been telling you for years, honey. But you're supposed to add, 'may his soul rest in peace' after speaking ill of the dead."

"Jake, sometimes you are impossible. But I have to admit, you were right about Vinny.'

"Forgive me for the trip to the Grand Canyon and making him sick?"

"Yes, I do, may his soul rest in peace."

"I am going to take Jasmine for a short walk before supper. See you in about 15 minutes."

"Take your time. Supper will be in half an hour."

After supper, the Lowens watched some TV and Samantha checked on Leila who had been fed a full liquid diet by her nurse.

"Leila is taking more nourishment now, the nurse thinks she'll be on solids and not need the IV in few days."

"That's great. Has the bodyguard shift changed?"

"Yes, they worked out an arrangement where the replacement calls the duty guard when he is at the door. Their phones are on vibrate so as not to disturb Leila or us when they witch. Tony wants the door locked at all times, he's very cautious. He also declined the ffer of a key, not wanting to have a lot of keys floating around. Same with the nurses. 'he night nurse rings on the cell phone Tony provided the nurses, so someone can let her 1."

It does feel like Grand Central Station, Sam. Did you give Holly a key?"

I did, but she knows about Tony's arrangements and doesn't want to use it tonight when he gets back. Tony's duty guard will let her in."

ake rubbed his chin. "I think I'll wait up for her. I want to hear what she has to say about he evening."

3ecause of the lack of sleep the night before, Samantha went to bed early while Jake lozed in the recliner. Samantha told Jake that he should rename it his sleep chair as he usually nodded off in it.

itirred out of a dreamless sleep, Jake heard the front door being opened. Tony came in to :heck with his guard and get a report on Leila, while Holly joined Jake and Jasmine in he family room.

'Hi, Uncle Jake, sorry to wake you."

'That's okay, I wasn't really asleep, just resting my eyes."

_etting that comment pass and ignoring the opportunity to ask if he always snored when 1e was just resting his eyes, Holly continued. "Aunt Samantha in bed?"

'Yeah, she was really tired after last night. Aren't you?"

'Extremely tired and a good dinner accompanied by a fine wine is not making me any nore awake."

=rom the hallway, Tony wished them good night and they heard the front door close)ehind him.

'How was it?"

'The meal was delicious, Tony is quite the gourmet. And you were right. He knows a lot about history. He told me of his educational plans, how he's completing his _indergraduate degree and his desire to go on to graduate studies."

'Did he ask you about yourself?"

'Yes, he's quite the gentleman. He didn't monopolize the conversation but asked about me. I was able to answer honestly about my childhood and education since I really did grow up in New Jersey and my mother is not Chinese American like my father is. I stayed away from reference to you and Samantha lest I get into a situation where I contradicted myself. He is a good listener, but an even better questioner. He wanted all the details about the break-in next door."

"What did you tell him?"

"Not much more than he could learn from the newspaper account. I did mention the shot taken at you, but I didn't say anything about it being silenced. I also left off that both of us were armed and could have shot back. He was particularly interested if Jasmine was alright. Said he's a big dog lover and would have hated to see her injured. He particularly asked if I knew if she had any ill effects today."

"Jasmine was lethargic early in the day, a little like she'd been drugged. I put it down to the excitement, but I'm not so sure whoever broke in didn't give her a treat that had a tranquilizer."

"Did he say anything about the photo he saw on my desk?"

"Totally mum. He didn't let on that he had any idea of who lived next door, but he did keep repeating that he was glad his guys were on duty. I decided to go out on limb and asked if he and his team were armed. He admitted they were. They have concealed carry permits from Florida and Arizona honors those permits, so they are legal."

"Did you ask him if he was armed while you were out to dinner?"

"I did and he said that Vitello required them to be armed at all times when on assignment."

"Wouldn't he have been surprised to look into your handbag and see you were also armed?"

Holly laughed. "I'm sure he would have been. I did ask him what kind of guns they carried. Told him you had made me a junior gun nut."

Jake smiled, "Thanks for putting the blame on me."

Holly ignored the jibe. "They're armed with a variety of weapons, depending on what they are wearing. Mostly they like .357 revolvers, especially the short barreled kind. But they also have .380 pocket autos for times when they need to go small and, get this, 9 mm pistols with high capacity magazines."

"Bingo, wonder if you guys could get a warrant to search the trailer or their cars?"

"Probably, but I doubt it would do any good. The silencers are probably well hidden, maybe in a bank box or some other offsite location. Ditto with the gun that was fired last ight. Tony is a smart boy. If he or one of his team discharged a weapon, that weapon is owhere near here, it could be in a box on its way back to Chicago. I don't think that they ould take a chance on dumping it anywhere it might be found."

I'm sure you are right, Holly. That is if Tony and his crew did the break-in. We just eed to keep an eye on them. Do you think we could get a bug in the trailer?"

We should have thought of that before they moved in, but Tony mentioned in passing at his guys are trained in detecting bugs. They regularly sweep rooms that his boss has eetings in for listening devices, I'm pretty certain that he would've done the same in ny place they are staying. Replaying it in my mind now, I wonder if he didn't interject at little piece of information for my benefit. Do you think my cover is blown?"

Not by us. Has your room been searched?"

I'm pretty sure it hasn't, anyway my guns are well hidden when I am not in the room or arrying them. The same with my badge."

Nevertheless, we better be on our guard."

Well, Uncle Jake, I'm calling it a night. Jasmine, sleep well and don't wake us tonight or an adventure."

Chapter Twenty Eight

The next several days saw a marked improvement in Leila's condition. She regained strength rapidly as though Samantha's presence acted as a tonic. Even Jake noticed that she seemed freer than she'd been when he had seen her with Vinny. Samantha, supplemented with photos provided by Vitello, told Leila about Vinny's funeral. Leila expressed pleasure that Vinny had gotten a good sendoff. He had always commented on the funerals of others and had told her he wanted an impressive funeral to demonstrate how important he was or rather, Leila said, had been. She confided to Samantha that Vinny felt inferior to Vitello and was always trying to score big to impress his older brother. Usually these ventures ended with Vitello bailing Vinny out. Much to Samantha's surprise, Leila told her that she kept the family checkbook and paid all the bills.

"Vinny always made out in public that I was stupid and that I should be glad he married me, but in truth, I was the one who could balance the family accounts. Vitello made him give over control of our money when he realized I wasn't the dumb broad that Vinny made me out to be. Vitello figured unless I did the accounts, he was condemned to always bailing Vinny out. And the dry cleaners he had set him up with did too well to let him squander the money. Of course, I knew they used the business to launder their money. Vinny used to joke when he was in his cups that he cleaned more than clothes in his business. I was a fool to marry him, but it promised a way out of the life I was living. And, God rest his soul, he could be charming when he wanted to be. It was just that lately, he didn't want to, at least with me. I told you that he had other women he must have charmed."

"How are you going to live, Leila?"

Leila smiled and her face actually seemed to light up. "No problem there, I managed to pay down the mortgage on the house. We, or rather I own it free and clear. It was in my name from the beginning for tax purposes. Paying it down early was just a matter of moving the money around and not letting Vinny blow it on the ponies or his floozies and of course lately, in the casinos ringing Chicago. I have also managed to set aside a decent nest egg. Vitello called yesterday and told me that the family would be providing me with a nice monthly income. I think I'll move to Florida, I always hated the cold. The heat doesn't bother me and if the summers get too hot there, I can always travel. Vinny left me alone and since we didn't have children, I started taking classes at the community college. After getting my associate's, I enrolled as a mature student at Dominican University and earned my bachelor's degree a year ago. My professors encouraged me to keep studying. Maybe I will."

Samantha looked at her old friend with new eyes. Leila, the ugly duckling who'd been picked on by the other girls at school, who had married badly and never had children, had truly turned into a swan. Samantha wasn't sure if she was feeling pride at having befriended her or gratitude to God for His mercy on Leila's life. Probably both. She

hought of the phrase her own father used to say, 'If life hands you a lemon, make
:monade.' Leila had surely borne out her father's proverb.

Leila, that's great! I'm so happy for you!"

Thanks, Samantha. It was your initial encouragement and friendship over all these years
nat was the one constant in my life, beside my faith in God. I often wondered if you
vere an angel sent by God to help me."

,amantha laughed. "I don't think Jake or the kids would think I'm an angel, but thanks
nyway."

ust then Jake poked his head in the door. "Hi, Leila, and Sam is wrong. I do think she's
n angel and I know the kids feel the same way. You're looking better today."

'Hi, Jake, thanks. How's your writing going?"

'As usual stuck on a problem of how to get my hero, or in this case, my heroine out of
ome jam I stuck them in. I'm taking a break to let my little grey cells rest before they
>ecome overheated and decided I would look in on you two or rather you four," nodding
o the day nurse and Larry who was on duty.

'Leila, do you remember anything at all about the day Vinny was killed?" asked
,amantha.

'Like I told the deputy sheriff, my mind is a blank from the time I answered the knock on
he door until I woke up from the coma in the hospital. The doctor said it was a way the
>rain had of dealing with trauma."

'ake shook his head in agreement. "Same thing can happen to soldiers in battle. They
lon't remember what happened. The can even forget acts of extreme bravery, though
hat is less common. What do you remember of the night before?"

'Vinny came back to the hotel extremely agitated. He tried to call Vitello but was put off
>y his assistant. Vinny fumed that Vitello was out with his mistress again and couldn't be
listurbed. I knew Vinny was ticked because he never before admitted to me that Vitello
ad a mistress. He was so mad he let it slip that he had a mistress too. He spouted, 'When
'm with Chloe and he wants me, he insists I come to the phone!' He didn't even realized
vhat he was saying but it confirmed my suspicions. I'm pretty sure I even know who this
Chloe is."

'Leila, I'm so sorry…"

Brushing off Samantha's sympathy with a wave of her hand, Leila continued. "It doesn't
matter now, does it? But Vinny was not only agitated, he was scared. He wouldn't tell
me who frightened him, wouldn't even admit he was frightened, pretended to be angry.

But I knew him too well, he was scared. Wouldn't go out for dinner, insisted on room service. Made me taste everything first. Claimed it was to be sure that there wasn't too much salt but he didn't fool me. He was afraid of being poisoned. What a bastard he was, may his soul rest in peace! Made me sleep on the sofa in the sitting room, said his back was bothering him and he didn't want the bed to sag under my weight. He was just scared that someone would break in and he wanted me to get it first. Insisted we order room service for breakfast. We had the first flight he could find us seats on for around midday."

Jake asked, "Did he try to call Vitello again?"

"No, he was afraid to call from the room. If Vitello called, he would have used some sor of code with him."

"Why didn't he use his cell phone?"

"That's the joke of it. He forgot the charger. Blamed me up and down for not packing it for him, but he hadn't given it to me to pack. Left it at work like he usually does. Anyway the cell phone was out of a charge and he couldn't find another charger for his phone. It's the latest, he always needed the latest and couldn't find one in Phoenix. Blamed that on me as well, claimed it was my idea to come to Arizona."

"Was it your idea?"

"No, Samantha, it was his. Some friend of his praised the climate up and down, shamed him into coming for a vacation. Vinny was always easily led. I was glad because I wanted to see your new house. I knew I would miss you after you moved."

Jake marveled at the woman who was talking. Was this the same quiet suppressed person he had seen so many times? Apparently so, but one who was careful not to let her light shine too brightly in front of her husband. Jake felt anger welling up inside him and wished he had made Vinny even sicker on the road to the Grand Canyon. Hell, he wished he had pushed him over the edge, which would have been difficult since Vinny was passed out across the seat while he and the women were looking at the canyon. For a brief moment, he felt a debt of gratitude to the person who murdered Vinny, but then realized the same cold blooded killer had used Leila as a shield and then tried to kill her.

Leila continued. "I ordered room service for breakfast, I wanted bacon and eggs, but Vinny insisted we both have pancakes. Harder to poison I suppose. I went toward the door and well, that's all I remember."

"Leila, I'm so sorry, I never realized how bad things were for you."

"That's okay Samantha. As your dad used to say, 'What doesn't kill you only makes you stronger.' I am a lot stronger than I was when we were in school and even this has made me stronger. Jake, when I am better, would you teach me to shoot a gun?"

Sure, Leila, but …"

But why? Because I want to defend myself. I know you taught Samantha to shoot, idn't you?"

amantha, still smiling because of Leila's reference to one of her father's proverbs, nswered for Jake. "He did, Leila, and is in fear for his life if he doesn't walk the straight nd narrow, aren't you, dear?"

Blushing in spite of himself, Jake responded. "Well, yes, plus I really love you, Sam. anyway Leila, hurry up and get well. I'll be glad to teach you. We can go to the range ogether with Samantha and she can show off her prowess."

Relating the conversation to Holly later that day, Jake commented they were no further long in figuring out who killed Vinny than they had been. It had all the earmarks of a professional hit, albeit one hastily arranged. Jake asked Holly if there was any progress on the search for Cindy and Harold.

It's like their car fell off the edge of the earth. Obviously, we haven't looked everywhere, Jake, but no one's seen it where we would have expected it to turn up."

The problem is that the car itself is so generic, a Chevrolet Impala, and the police can't top every one of them on the road."

"That is the problem," agreed Holly.

Puzzled by the strange look on Jake's face, Holly asked. "Are you in pain, is something wrong?"

"Apart from my being an idiot, no. Holly is the warrant Tom got to search the place next door still valid?"

"If it isn't, he can get another one. Why?"

"Did anyone check the plates on Bowden's car? The owner of the house left her car in he garage, which was why the Rousseaus always had at least one car in the driveway. I till wonder about the fourth car that was in the garage next to Bowden's car. I'm kicking myself for not realizing the significance of that car earlier. I didn't get a good enough look at it to determine if it was Willie Carlinski's car from Chicago."

"You told us that before, but why check the plates on Bowden's car?"

'To see if they are still on the car, Holly, to see if they are still on the car!"

127

Holly dialed Tom who quickly agreed to ask Deputy Lodestone to check if the vehicle parked in the garage still had its plates. Within 15 minutes, a Sheriffs' car was parked next door and a pair of deputies were seen entering the house. Exiting in less than five minutes, it was all of sixty seconds before Jake's cell phone rang.

"You were right, Dr. Lowen, the plate from the car parked in the garage is missing. We're running a check on the owner's registration number and will be revising our all points bulletin as soon as we get the plate number. Good work, sir. We should have spotted it when we searched the house. Maybe one of the guys did and just thought that the owner had hidden the plates to keep someone from driving her car. We have heard of snow birds doing just that and then forgetting to reinstall them on the car when they return. They're often indignant when our guys pull them over for not having a license plate."

Chapter Twenty Nine

ake was getting ready to take Jasmine for her morning walk when Holly came into the itchen.

"Can I join you, Jake?"

"Sure, Holly. Jasmine is always glad for more company. I think she finds my onversation on historical topics rather boring at times."

Iolly laughed. "Your sense of humor comes out in your novels, as well as in person."

"You've read one of my novels?"

"Aunt Samantha lent me several, it's good writing. I really like history. By the way, so loes Tony. He's been reading some of your books as well, but he is getting them from 3arnes and Noble, not Samantha."

"Great, anything to increase my royalties, even having Chicago mobsters camped in my lriveway."

Iolly laughed again.

Nhen they were well out of earshot of the house, Holly took the conversation on a erious turn. "Tom called early this morning. They found Harry Gianelli's body."

"What! Where?"

"Outside of Tombstone. He was shot execution style in the back. They haven't finished he autopsy yet, but preliminary examination indicates two bullet wounds in the back at airly close range, followed by a coupe de grace to the back of the head. He was killed vhere they found the body, the blood pooling under it marks it as the murder site."

"How long was he dead?"

"At least two days, maybe three. Could even be longer."

"Where was he found?"

"He had rented a cabin in the area. It was a self service cabin. No maid service so no one :ame in on a regular basis. His rental period was up, owner came to collect the key iguring he had cleared out and just left the key in the cabin. Found him on the floor."

"What other details did Tom have?"

"He said the owner was positive the door was locked, had to use his passkey to get in. Looked like he had been killed fairly soon after he moved in, bed wasn't slept in. They knew it was Harry from the driver's license and other papers he had on him."

"Was his wallet in his pocket?"

"Jake, no wonder you are a good writer, you think like a detective. No, the wallet was next to the body, his pockets had all been gone through, nothing else on him. No gun or money."

"Where has our boy been for the last three months since he disappeared from Chicago? Couldn't have been at the cabin. Any car outside?"

"No, and no luggage in the cabin. If it wasn't for the blood under the body, our guys would be tempted to think he was killed somewhere else and dumped there. But it's tough, if not impossible, to replicate the bleed marks. No, Harry Gianelli was killed where they found the body."

"But why not kill him in the desert and figure his body would never be found, why leave his body where it would be found at the end of the rental?"

"That's what Tom is asking, Jake. It was like whoever killed him wanted him to be found."

"Are they sure that it is Harry?"

"They ran his prints, the bureau had had him fingerprinted when they started to run him as an informant. He wasn't happy but agreed."

"What about his features? Did they recognize him?"

"The head wound blew away part of his face, actually until we get the lab results, it migh have been more than one shot to the head. But one thing was strange, though. He was wearing his hair shorter. Harry was always vain about his hair, always combing it. The stiff with Harry's prints was wearing a crew cut."

"A crew cut? Holly do you think I could see the body?"

"They're doing the autopsy in Tucson. That is the seat of the jurisdiction area in which he was found. I'm not sure where they will take the body next. His death blows the conspiracy and corruption case that Justice was building against some key political figures in Illinois."

"Was he the only witness?"

"No, but he was the star witness and the real kingpin. Everything revolved around him."

I'm sorry for your team, and I'm sorry for the people of Illinois, they deserve better government than they have had. Can you call Tom and arrange for me to see the body of Gianelli in Tucson, Holly?"

I'll call him and arrange for us to see the body, Uncle Jake."

After a quick breakfast, Holly and Jake took off in Jake's Jeep. Samantha elected to stay home and be with Leila. The official story for Tony and whoever else that asked was that Jake was doing some research for his next novel which had some of the setting in southern Arizona and Holly volunteered to come along. Jasmine, seeing Jake take off in the Jeep, figured he was going into the mountains and whined to go along. Tony, coming off a shift, heard Jasmine and asked Samantha what was wrong.

Jake usually takes her when he goes off in the Jeep, but this time he is doing some research that required him to leave her home."

Can I take her for a run? I need to do my morning run."

Sure, if you think she'll go with you."

Let's see. Come here, girl. Want to go for a run?"

As though she understood, Jasmine enthusiastically thumped her tail on the floor.

Interesting Tony, Jasmine's always friendly but she is pretty much Jake's dog. She has even hesitated to go with my niece, Holly, who she knows. You must have a way with dogs."

Thanks, but my real secret is I always have dog biscuits in my pocket. Never know when you'll need to charm a threatening dog."

After they left, Samantha made a mental note to report this conversation to Jake and Holly.

131

Chapter Thirty

On the two hour drive to Tucson, Jake and Holly compared notes. He learned more about the double cross Gianelli had pulled, thumbing his nose at both the mob and the Feds. He managed to lie low, in spite of the best efforts of the FBI to find him. They knew the mob had tried as well, witness the dispatch of Willie Carlinski, AKA Willie the Cook. With the apparent discovery of Harry's body, it seemed more likely the body Jasmine had uncovered was Carolyn Gianelli. But where was Willie the Cook? Had Harry managed to kill the mob hit man? Had he been bought off with some of the money Harry had stolen? Was the body they were going to see really that of Harry Gianelli? Holly mentioned how difficult it is to fake fingerprints.

Having discussed the case, she changed the topic.

"If you were really my uncle, I would ask you for advice, Jake. I'm trying to decide what to do. I have been in the bureau for nearly ten years and I don't know if I want to make this my life career. My life isn't turning out like I thought it would."

"What did you think would happen, Holly?"

"Well, I was pretty programmed to go to college. Law school seemed natural since I didn't know what else to do. After law school I got recruited by the bureau because they needed some Asian Americans to work undercover. It was exciting work and I really liked what I was doing. It was dangerous, so this overprotected Asian-American suburban girl finally got the excitement she secretly craved. But ..."

"But undercover work made having a normal dating relationship difficult, if not impossible. You could never meet the right type of guy."

"Wow! How did you know that?"

"Easy, I have the same problem when I write my Civil War spy novels. My characters, male and female, can't find the right person. In a novel it adds interest. In real life it means heartaches."

"I wish you really were my uncle. You seem to understand." Holly hesitated before going on.

"Like Tony?"

"Yes, Jake. Like Tony. He's funny, intelligent, charming, polite, good looking, just the kind of fellow a girl wants to take home to meet her parents, except ..."

"Except he is a mobster and may have tried to kill my next door neighbor and taken a shot at me, though I still think whoever shot at me purposely missed. The shooter was

ounting on my putting my head down and not returning fire. Which is exactly what I
id."

And the shooter didn't know I was with you and had a .40 Smith and Wesson but held
ff shooting because I couldn't get a clear shot in the dark."

And Tony didn't meet you until the following morning. You were already in bed when
e came by to check things out and noticed the photo of Harold Rousseau. But back to
our dilemma."

Well, my mom, who I don't have to remind you is not Samantha's sister, keeps bugging
e to get married and settle down. She is constantly going 'tick-tock' when I call her on
e phone."

That must be annoying!"

It is, but the truth is I would like to get married. It is lonely on the road and I long for a
lace to call home, like you and Samantha have. It's been great staying with you. But I
ink I probably need to quit the Bureau."

What about a desk job?"

I thought of that, but what I think I should do is practice corporate law and if I find the
ight guy, settle down and work part-time. That is kind of work you can do part-time. I
ad a woman professor who did that while her kids were young and then took a position
t the law school. She still is a partner in a firm."

What's holding you back?"

I don't know. Fear, inertia, lack of opportunity. No, that last one isn't true. I have had
pportunities."

Holly, if you were my niece, I would tell you to follow your heart. Down deep you
now what you want to do, peel away the layers of fear, parental pressure, even societal
ressure and find what you really want to do inside. What you will find is God's will for
ou. When you find it ask God for the courage to do it."

Thanks, Jake. I'll try to do that."

ulling up outside the Tucson morgue, they were met by Tom Roberts.

He's not pretty. They cleaned him up, but the face is still pretty shot away. As I told
ou on the phone, we made the positive ID by his prints."

eading them into the hygienic bowels of the building, Jake marveled again at how
terile the environment seemed. Not at all like a morgue in the Civil War where bodies

and body parts were stacked every which way. The stench of those morgues was overwhelming, forcing workers to hold scented handkerchiefs to their noses to ward off the smell of death. This place reeked of disinfectant, an odor that made Jake nauseous.

Resisting the impulse to gag, Jake allowed himself to be led to the slab on which the body of Harry Gianelli lay. At Tom's signal, the morgue attendant pulled back the sheet.

"Oh, my God," cried out Jake. "I can solve the mystery of where Harry Gianelli has been for the last two months. He's been living next door to me in Scottsdale."

"Are you sure?" The question came from both Holly and Tom in almost precise synchronization. If it would not have been for their location and the reason for their question, no doubt all three would have broken out laughing. As it was Holly suppressed a smile.

"Positive, look at that birth mark on his right arm. It's a peculiar shape, like the head of stallion. I noticed it when we first met."

"But why didn't I recognize him from the photos from the casino?" asked Tom.

"He changed his hairstyle and facial features."

"How?"

"Hair style is easy, cut his hair and sport a crew cut. Color is easy with dye. Facial features with pads in his checks to make him look fatter. To finish the effect, an inflatable tube around his stomach. When I first met him, I was struck by his pudginess but how fit his arms looked. I have a hunch that his legs were being concealed behind baggy pants. Harry Gianelli was a fit man who used stage makeup to alter his appearance. Change of hairstyle and color, change of his features, and a change of clothing style. Harry was a flashy dresser, Harold was definitely the three piece suit type. You probably never saw him in short selves, did you Tom?"

"Come to think of it, Jake, I hadn't. But how do you know about all this changing of appearance stuff?"

"In my first teaching job, I was in charge of the drama department. I had a theatre minor as an undergrad. I am not sure if it was my interest in theatre or my love of history that led me to Civil War reenacting. Probably both, after all these reenactments are nothing else but theatre played outdoors with cannon and rifles. Anyway, over the years I learned a lot about makeup. I should have seen it on Harold, but then I never saw him as Harry before today. That is also why the grainy photos of Harry and the casino photos of Harold didn't ring any alarm bells."

"But you said Tony LaMotte recognized Harold's photo on your desk. How do you explain that? queried Holly.

'I think it was his eyes. We were fooled because Harold was wearing color contacts. We were looking for someone with bright blue eyes. Harold was using contacts that made his eyes appear brown. But the photo Tony saw was in black and white, he recognized the shape of Harry's eyes. And if I am not mistaken, one of the photos showed Harry in short sleeves, we need to look at it again and see if the birthmark is visible. If it is, it would have been a dead giveaway to Tony who is a very observant lad. If you could get him to walk the straight and narrow, he would be a useful addition to your agency. I am guessing that he called Vitello and Vitello ordered a hit to take place right away, before Leila was moved in." Jake had the look of a man who had solved a difficult puzzle.

"Because Harry killed his brother?" asked Holly.

"I don't think Vitello knows everything we know about that. Vinny didn't dare leave a message for Vitello on who he saw. It's probable that it was Harry Vinny identified. No, Vitello had another reason to have Tony and his team kill Harry. Vitello wanted to keep Harry from testifying. If it turns out that Harry did kill Vinny and I'm not sure how you will make that case, Vitello will be happy to have scored a two for one kill. At, least that's my guess, " offered Jake.

"Jake, are you saying this was a mob hit?"

"Tom, you and Holly are the professionals, what do you think?"

Holly, who had been following this exchange with rapt attention, spoke up. "Whoever killed Harry, it was someone he trusted enough to turn his back on. Where is Cindy?"

"Do you think Cindy killed him? You had lunch with her, Holly. Does she strike you as a murderer?"

"Jake, you of all people asking that question! Samantha was telling me the other day that you're always telling her that the best spies don't look like spies. She said that she wondered sitting by Leila's bedside if the best murderers don't look like murderers. I think Cindy might well be capable of pulling the trigger on Harry or Harold. And besides that, where is she?"

Tom added to the list of unanswered questions. "And how did Harry get to the cabin. Where is the car they rented? It is possible that we may still find Cindy's body and someone else did this. For all we know, the killer followed Harry and Cindy, killed Harry and abducted Cindy."

"But why? Why not just kill them both?"

It was Jake who posed an answer, not Tom. "Because Cindy knows where the money is stashed. She was taken by the killer or killers to recover the money. Let's assume it was a mob hit. You both agree that Harry Gianelli was vital to the government's corruption case. Job one, take out Harry. Job two, recover the money. Harry, if he really killed Carlinski and his wife, is a dangerous man. Too dangerous to take along on a mission to retrieve the money. But if Cindy knows where he stashed it, she would presumably be easier to control. Perhaps they promised her a cut and told her they would let her go when she took them to the loot. They wouldn't of course. They couldn't afford to let her go but she might not figure that out. Anyway it was her only chip. Thinking back to the night of the break-in at the Rousseau house, they probably would have killed Harry and then sweated the location of what's left of the money from Cindy."

Holly and Tom nodded in agreement. "We can put out an APB for Cindy Rousseau."

"Go to her web site, Tom. There are some great photos of her on it."

Chapter Thirty One

On the drive back to Phoenix, Holly's cell phone rang. She mostly listened, punctuated by noises that indicated to the other party she was following the conversation.

Just before hanging up, she said, "Great! Thanks for calling. I'll tell Jake."

"Tell me what?"

"Do you play the lottery?"

"I occasionally buy a ticket when the Powerball goes over $100 million, why?"

"Buy one today. We are two for two. The rental car, the one with Mrs. Bowden's license plate on it turned up in the long term parking at the Las Vegas airport."

"Why am I not surprised? Vegas has figured in this story from the beginning. When was it left there?"

"Can't be determined. Since it was in long term parking, they don't make the sweeps as often as they do in the short term lot. And the car was backed into the space so the plate wasn't visible on a drive through. It was only when we indicated on the APB that the plate was from Arizona did they check on foot. And before you ask, the parking ticket was not in the car. They have towed the car to a garage where it is getting a thorough going over. One thing I can tell you, no visible blood stains on the seat or in the trunk. The crime lab boys will check for any traces of blood."

"Probably no surveillance cameras captured the car being parked."

"Unfortunately correct. And no Cindy Rousseau renting a car. However we can't be sure that she didn't rent something under another name. What do you think?"

"Holly, you are the FBI special agent, I'm just a has-been history professor in early retirement. What do I know?"

"Jake, I am starting to have more sympathy with Samantha when she complains about you. You just broke our case by making an identification of Harold Rousseau as Harry Gianelli. Every suggestion or idea you have made has proven correct. And you are far from being a 'has been.' I saw you teaching those agents at the range. You had them eating out of your hand. Samantha told me you won several teaching awards. What do you think?"

"It would be a waste to travel to Las Vegas. Cindy isn't there."

"Do you think she flew out already?"

"I think she is headed back to Arizona, specifically to the house next door, to pick up her mail and get her new passport. I wouldn't be surprised if she picks it up at the Post Office. Can you call Tom and have the Post Office that services our subdivision staked out. I would suggest she be picked up when she collects her mail."

After Holly made the call to Tom and got his agreement with Jake's suggestion, she turned to Jake and asked, "How did you figure that out?"

"If I'm right, it's simple. One, we know at some point, Harry or Harold traveled in the Chevy Impala, probably hiding out here and there and eventually arriving at the cabin. They could have switched cars but wouldn't know about the attempt on their lives so had no reason to believe we would know they were using Bowden's license plate. They figured they were in clear, though they would avoid all traffic stops because they wouldn't want the plate run on a cop's computer. Two, whoever killed Harry was someone he trusted enough to turn his back on. That person or persons were with Harry when he collected the money, or knows where he stashed it. After all twenty million is a lot of paper to carry around. I don't think Harry had it all at the house. But I think this little trip was a cash gathering expedition. Bundle up the cash, change it into bigger notes or wire it to an off shore bank, that kind of stuff. The crime scene guys didn't find any trace of money in the house, did they?"

"Only one wrapper that came from a bundle of hundreds. It had fallen behind the dresser and was missed by the Rousseaus, if they were even looking for it. As it was, our guys had to move the dresser to get it."

"I'll take that as confirmation of my thesis. Where was I? Oh, yes, point three. Cindy, if she is still alive, will be picking up the passports and eventually making her way out of the country with the money. If Cindy is dead, we may have lost the trail, but can you have Tom and the Bureau check on people renting safety deposit boxes in, say, the last four months?"

"That's a tall order, I don't know how we can do it, even with our resources."

"You don't need to check them all, only the banks that have rented out large boxes. Those don't rent as often and most banks only have a few. If you needed those boxes, you might need to go to several banks in a town to find an empty box."

"I'll get right on it. And make sure Tom has an APB out for Cindy. I wonder if we'll find her alive."

But it turned out Cindy found them, and more specifically, Jake. And she was very much alive.

Chapter Thirty Two

ate the next evening, Jasmine set up a ferocious barking. Sam, Jake and Holly had been relaxing in the family room watching an old movie on the TV.

ooking over at the women, Jake said, "Wait here, I'm going to check out what going on."

"I'll come with you. It sounds like it's coming from the direction of the Rousseaus," said Holly.

topping in his study to get his revolver, Jake glanced over his shoulder to see Holly with er .357 revolver in her hand.

Where did that come from?"

They don't call it a concealed weapon for no reason, Jake. I've been carrying my revolver with me since the last break-in and before you ask, I have my shield under my hirt."

ake saw that Holly had tucked her t-shirt into her pants to reveal her badge clipped to he belt of her jeans. He supposed her revolver had been resting in the holster that he ould see next to the badge.

Slick, Holly, I hadn't noticed."

Quietly slipping out the kitchen door, they made their way alongside the Lowens' garage. asmine had already charged ahead, eluding Jake's attempt to grab her collar.

roceeding cautiously, Jake noted that Jasmine had reached the Rousseau's garage but topped barking. Worried about his beloved pet, Jake raced across the space between the wo houses, only to find Tony petting Jasmine by the back door of the garage.

Tony, what's going on?"

"I heard something over here, Dr. Lowen. Since we know that the house is empty, I ame over to check it out."

"How long have you been here?" asked Holly, making no attempt to holster her revolver or conceal her badge.

"Just before Jasmine. I was in the Airstream and heard something. As I stepped out, I heard Jasmine barking. She has better ears than I do and got suspicious first."

"Have you been inside?" asked Holly.

"No, not yet."

"Wait here with Jasmine while Jake and I go in."

"Don't you want help?"

"I'm an FBI agent, Tony. This is official business. On second thought, take Jasmine back to the house and call for backup."

"With all due respect, Holly. Maybe Tony should use his cell phone to call 911 from here and keep Jasmine with him. She might prove useful if we find someone inside or need to look for someone inside."

"Okay, but I go in first, Jake, cover me."

Flipping on lights as they went in, Jake and Holly made a throughout search.

"Someone came in through the kitchen door. Stuff was piled up there after the crime scene guys went through and it was knocked over. That's what Jasmine heard, this pile of stuff failing down."

"I think you're right Holly, but it looks like they left through the patio slider. It's on the other side and Tony won't have noticed them go if they were still inside."

"Do you think Tony or one of his guys killed Harry?"

"No chance, Holly, Samantha said that they were all accounted for. None were missing long enough to drive to Tombstone."

"Well, that's a relief."

"What are you going to tell Tony about your being an agent?"

"That I'm taking a break from a bad marriage and that I had accumulated leave time, but I'm required to carry my weapon and badge 24/7."

"Sounds good, let's call him and Jasmine. She is a trained search and rescue dog. If there is a body here, living or dead, she'll find it."

Jasmine had just started her search when the deputy sheriff arrived. On Jake's command, Jasmine searched the whole house but came up empty. Leaving the deputy to again secure the house as a crime scene and being told the crime scene team would come in the morning to dust the place again for prints, Jake and Holly returned home. After assuring Samantha that all three of them were alright and that Jasmine again played the hero, they decided to call Tony in and confront him with his probable recognition of Harold as arry. While Jasmine had been conducting her search, Holly called Tom Roberts who rived just as they were ready to call Tony in. Jake went around to the trailer and asked ony to come into the house.

nce inside, he politely inquired "How can I help you Dr. Lowen?"

Tony, this is Special Agent Tom Roberts of the FBI. Holly Tan is also a special agent."

Pleased to meet you sir." To Holly he said, "I knew there was something special about ou."

Iolly took the lead in asking the questions. "Tony, you identified the photo you saw on Ir. Lowens' desk as Harry Gianelli, didn't you?"

ausing a moment to consider his answer, Tony replied. "I was pretty sure it was him. he eyes were the same, but the birth mark on his arm was a dead giveaway. I asked Iarry about it once and he said it was because he was Italian. An Italian stallion eferring to his sexual prowess. Begging your pardon, Holly, that is Special Agent Tan."

Why didn't you tell Dr. Lowen?"

How did I know that Dr. Lowen knew anything about Harry or that you Feds were ooking for him? I didn't want to complicate his life needlessly. And remember Special Agent Tan, I didn't know you were an FBI agent until tonight."

Breaking in, Tom asked. "You could have called the local office of the FBI."

As it says in the Good Book, Proverbs 26:17, 'He who passes by and meddles in a uarrel not his own is like one who takes a dog by the ears."

What version is that, Tony?"

New King James. My mother, even though she was a Catholic and raised us Catholic, nade us go to the Holiness Baptist Church Sunday School and Youth Group. She felt we eeded a better grasp of the Bible than we were getting in our parish. So my three rothers and I learned a lot of Scripture. Kind of sticks with you. Especially that verse ince I am such a dog lover, always have been and I knew before I read that verse that it vasn't right to pick up a dog by its ears. But I don't imagine you have me here for a Bible lesson."

Trying to get back on track, Holly asked. "Did you call Vitello Espennelli?"

"Mr. Espennelli requires me to report in every evening. I have been doing that since this ssignment began, more frequently if Mrs. Espennelli's condition changed. I might have nentioned it to him."

"Might?"

"I honestly don't remember, Agent Roberts."

Desperately, Tom asked. "Did you shoot at Dr. Lowen?"

Tony looked honestly offended. "I would never harm Dr. or Mrs. Lowen. I am a body guard, not an assassin."

In one final attempt to shake Tony, Holly asked. "Did you know Harry Gianelli is dead?"

"No I didn't. May his soul rest in peace. How did he die?"

"He was executed, shot in the back and in the head." said Tom.

"Harry was not the best of men and not very nice to people, but nobody deserves to die like that." commented Tony.

Tom asked if either Holly or Jake had any more questions and seeing them both shake their heads no, dismissed Tony.

After he left, Jake asked, "Should you have told him not to tell Vitello?"

"Doesn't matter, it will be in tomorrow's paper. What do you make of his story Holly?"

"Apart from not remembering if he told Vitello, I think he stuck to the truth. I believe he told Vitello and Vitello sent in a team. Tony might have been on it as the outside guard i he didn't want to be an assassin."

"What about his story of not wanting to hurt Jake?"

Holly laughed. "That's the easiest part, Tom. He didn't try to hurt Jake; he shot way over his head."

Chapter Thirty Three

arly the next morning, Jake was awakened by the jarring ring of the phone. Since he
was deep in a dream about the Civil War, the constant ringing fit into his dream as the
warning alarm being sounded by a sentry. Jake recalled being puzzled at the sound being
made by the soldier, and even more puzzled why the troops weren't responding to call to
arms signifying an imminent attack. Just as the first of the Confederate troops swept into
the sleeping Union troops, whooping and giving out the rebel yell, Jake finally awoke
from his dream and realized the ringing was the bedside telephone.

amantha, an unusually sound sleeper, only stirred in her sleep and rolled over as Jake
fumbled for the phone and muttered a sleepy, "Hello."

Dr. Lowen, I'm sorry if I woke you up, but it's urgent and I don't have anyone else to
urn to."

napping awake, Jake said. "Slow down. Who is this and what's the matter?"

It's Cindy Rousseau. I'm in trouble and I need your help. I'm so frightened!"

ake heard her muffled sobs on the other end of the phone. "Where are you?"

In a cheap motel in Phoenix. Harold dumped me at the Grand Canyon. I mean not in the
anyon but he left me in a motel where we were staying. I think he drugged my drink.
When I awoke about noon the next day, he was gone. I didn't have any money, he
actually took the money out of my purse, even my credit cards. I had to call a friend in
Vegas collect and ask her to wire me some money so I could pay the motel bill and get
back down here. It took days for this to happen and for me to find a way down to
Phoenix."

ully awake, Jake asked, "When did this happen?"

The day after we left, ten days ago. It has been horrible." The sobs increased in volume.

You have been stuck in the Grand Canyon for that whole time?"

Yes, I actually tried to get a job at the motel or one of the restaurants to make some
money, it was horrible, just horrible. A guy treated me to dinner then wanted me to go
with him to his room. I had to fight him off. I knew Harold was bad news but I wanted to
believe in him."

Did Harold ever tell you his real name, Cindy?"

There was a pregnant pause before Cindy spoke again. "Gianelli, Harold Gianelli."

Did Harold tell you why his was running away?"

"He was married to this horrible bitch, that's how he described her. But now I am not so sure. He was a real bastard himself. Maybe I should've had more sympathy with his wife."

"What are you going to do now?"

"Go back to Vegas and try to get my old job back or a job someplace else. Maybe as a cocktail waitress."

"How can I help you?"

"Like I said, Harold, the bastard, took all my money. I borrowed money to get here and need to pay it back."

"How much do you need? Maybe I can lend you some."

"Thanks, Dr. Lowen. That's very generous of you. But the reason I came here instead of going straight back to Vegas is because I have some money stashed here and it will be enough to settle with my friend and give me a small stake. I didn't trust Harold, I figured if he would cheat his wife, he would cheat me. I took some of the money he had and kept it for a rainy day. He was gambling so much and I was handling the finances, he never missed it."

"I still don't see how you need my help...."

Cindy interrupted Jake before he could finish. "The money is in a safety deposit box, but the key is in the house. I went there last night to get it but before I could a man with a gun came after me. Your dog saved me."

"Jasmine saved you? How?"

"Her barking distracted the man who turned to intercept the dog. He told me to stay put but I ran out the patio door. I felt something fly past my head, I think he shot at me."

"Were you hurt?"

"No, just scared out of my wits. I've never been so scared in my life."

"Did you get what you came for?"

"That's the problem, the man must have been watching the house. Before I could get the safe deposit box key from where I hid it, he had his gun on me. I think he would have killed me." The sobs which had diminished, increased again.

"What do you want me to do?"

If I told you where the key was, could you get it and bring it to me?"

Jake paused, more for effect than to consider the request. This could be the break the bureau was looking for. It might still leave Cindy high and dry, but she should have known that stealing another woman's man was wrong and stealing his 'ill-gotten' gains was also wrong. "Sure, I guess so. Just tell me where it is and where to meet you."

Cindy paused. "Let me call you back, say in an hour. Is that enough time?"

"Okay."

The key is inside a light switch in the guest bedroom on the left of the hall as you go toward the far side of the house from your home. There is a closet light switch, unscrew the cover and you'll see it."

"Got it, call me in an hour."

Hanging up the phone, Jake mused. So that is why the crime scene technicians didn't find it. They virtually tore the place apart looking in and under furniture, checking cushions and mattresses, cabinets and closets, but they probably never thought about checking under the cover plates since they were looking for money and weapons, not a safe deposit box key.

Dressing quickly, he went down the hall toward Holly's room. As he passed Leila room, he looked in to see the nurse dozing in a chair next to Leila's bed and the bodyguard reading a book. The nurse was due to go off duty in an hour and with the bodyguard awake he could alert the nurse to any stirring of the patient. Jake had noticed how the combination of nurses and bodyguards had learned to work together and complement each other.

Knocking lightly on Holly's door, he waited for her to respond.

"What's the matter, Jake?" whispered Holly, forgetting in the early morning to use her customary preface, "Uncle."

"Can you get dressed quickly and meet me in the kitchen? It's rather urgent. Bring your gun and cell phone."

Four minutes later, dressed in jeans and a T-shirt, her hair disheveled and without a trace of makeup, but armed and presumably dangerous, Holly appeared in the kitchen, where Jake was drinking a cup of coffee and eating one of Samantha's sweet rolls.

"What's up?"

Jake quickly filled her in on the phone call from Cindy.

145

"What are you going to do?"

"Retrieve the key."

"Should I call Tom?"

"Yes, but tell him to stay put, no sirens or lights. I wouldn't be surprised if Cindy called from a cell phone and is watching the house right now."

"Wow, Jake. You are suspicious of everyone."

"Never underestimate the depravity of man, Holly. Or for that matter the depravity of woman. I am going next door exiting our house from the front. You slip out the back and try to cross the space between the houses. I have looked out front, there is no car there or anywhere else that can get a line of sight on you if you go out the back and slip into the garage. I will go around the front, try the door and if it's locked, like it should be, make a show of going around to the back. Anyone watching will assume that I am going to try the kitchen door or the patio door. Meet me in the kitchen and kept your guard up."

Two minutes later, Jake strolled up to the front door of the Rousseaus which had been sealed and marked with fresh crime scene yellow tape from the incident of the night before. Finding the door secure, Jake walked around to the back where Holly let him in through the kitchen door.

"I had to force the back door to the garage again. Your poor neighbor, Mrs. Bowden, is going to need to replace that door. For safety she should replace it with a solid door and not one with half glass that is so easy to enter."

"I'll make a note to tell her. Watch my back while I find the key."

It took Jake less than a minute to uncover the switch and retrieve the key, heading back to the kitchen, he froze in his tracks when he heard Holly shout.

"Put up your hands and come out where I can see you or I'll shoot."

Flattening against the wall, Jake silently cursed himself for not bringing his revolver. I don't want to die like this, he thought, nor do I want Holly to die like this. Waiting for what would happen next, Jake realized that he was holding his breath. He let it out just as he heard male voice say, "Don't shoot. I'm coming out."

Jake recognized the voice as Larry's, one of Tony's bodyguard team.

Strolling into the kitchen, Jake saw Holly crouched behind the kitchen island, her .40 caliber pistol still trained on Larry.

What are you doing here?"

Tony told us to keep a watch on this house from the trailer and check on anything suspicious. I looked up and saw someone enter the house and came over to check it out."

Armed with a handgun?"

My gun is on the floor where I put it at your command. Would you mind not pointing yours at me? Tony requires us to be armed, we are bodyguards and someone did try to kill Mrs. Espennelli."

Okay, Larry. That's reasonable. Why did Tony tell you to watch this house?"

Well, he identified the guy who was living here as someone with mob connections and possibly dangerous. Apparently his former pals were after him. Tony was concerned for Mrs. Espennelli's safety and for the safety of Dr. and Mrs. Lowen. We're not just guarding Mrs. Espennelli."

Holstering her pistol, Holly dismissed Larry and asked Jake if he was done. Nodding, Holly said, "Let's get out of here. This place is starting to give me the creeps."

Back in the kitchen, having repeated their charade of Holly going in the back door while Jake again made a point of going in the front of his own home, Jake opened the little wallet supplied by the bank to hold the safety deposit box key.

Only one key. The bank usually supplies two keys for these boxes. Wonder where the other one is."

Maybe Cindy carried it with her and she lost it, or Harry stole it, Jake."

I don't think she's the kind to lose something like this and I don't think Harry stole it. It would be useless to anyone else for two reasons. Even though the name of the bank is on the envelope, the branch is not listed. There are a dozen branches in Phoenix alone, not to mention the rest of the state and this bank is popular all over the Western states. Second, you need to know the name the account is listed under and then have that signature match the signature card on file. If Harry did steal it, he would have tried to find out what she had in the box, maybe even force her to empty it. No, I think she hid the other key where he can't get to it and needed this one."

What in the world are you two doing up this early?"

Good morning, Samantha. Jake and I had an adventure, haven't we, Jake."

Holly got to draw her gun on one the bodyguards."

A look of shock crossed, Samantha's face. "Did one those guys try to enter your room?"

Laughing, Jake said. "No, you slept through a phone call from Cindy Rousseau asking me to retrieve a safe deposit box key from where she had hid it. I asked Holly to cover my back. Larry, acting on Tony's orders saw some suspicious movement and came over to check it out."

Quickly Jake filled Samantha in on Cindy's hard luck story and her instructions for retrieving the key and to wait for her further instructions.

Just then, the phone rang. Picking it up, the women heard Jake say that he had gotten it and then a series of yeses followed by a recitation of his cell phone number.

Hanging up, Jake looked puzzled. "There is a car parked at the end of the street. She wants me to walk there alone, get in the car and drive away. She said she would call me on my cell phone once I started driving on the 101."

"I'm coming with you."

"Me too," chimed in Holly.

"No, I think she is watching the house, she called shortly after I came back in."

"If she is watching the house, how did she get another car here?"

"She could have driven one, walked a few blocks, called cab and driven back in another car. The car she wants me to drive could be the one she used and left here last night."

"Or she could have an accomplice."

"Holly's right, she could be working with somebody, maybe whoever killed Harry. Jake don't do it."

"This key is our one link to Cindy. She knows more than she told us so far. Piecing together the stories she told us, including what she told Holly over lunch still leaves a lot of gaps. I have to go."

"Let us follow you in my car."

"No, just call Tom and Lodestone and give them a description of the car and the plate number. Holly, before I leave, take Jasmine for a run and memorize the plate number. Samantha, stay by the phone, including your cell. I'm going in a couple of minutes."

Holly and Jasmine left by the back door and were jogging around the corner when Jake appeared at the front door and kissed Samantha good bye. Samantha has seen Holly drop one knee before reaching the white Mazda sedan, ostensibly to tie her shoe lace, but really memorizing the plate number.

Walking slowly to the sedan, Jake felt the hair stand up on the back of his neck and wondered if this was how condemned prisoners feel as they make their last walk to the execution chamber. Getting in the driver's seat, Jake found the keys already in the ignition. He had glanced in the windows and saw the car was unoccupied though the deeply tinted windows made it hard to see clearly into the back seat. Using the pretext of adjusting the rearview mirror, he looked behind him to see a blanket crumpled up on the floor and the rear seat empty. He started the car up and headed for the 101.

As he passed the turnoff from the 101 for the casino at Talking Stick, he heard a voice from the back seat say, "Keep driving, Dr. Lowen."

Looking in the rear view mirror, he saw Cindy Rousseau. She was partly kneeling on the floor and partly sitting on the edge of the back seat. She must have been concealed under the blanket. The surprise of hearing her voice paled in comparison to the shock of seeing her point an automatic pistol at his head.

Hi, Cindy. What's with the subterfuge and the gun?"

You'll have to excuse me, Dr. Lowen, I just don't trust anyone anymore. It is merely a precaution against us being followed. Take the 202 exit heading east, then get on route 87 going north."

Following her instructions, Jake asked, "Where are we heading?"

You'll see, just drive."

Reaching a lonely spot on Route 87, Cindy directed Jake to pull over and get out of the car and to pop the trunk. "Leave the keys in the ignition."

When Jake was out of the car, Cindy said, "Hand over the bank box key."

Pocketing the key, Cindy motioned for Jake to move toward the partially opened trunk.

"Get in and put your hands behind your back."

"But it's in the high 80s already, it's going to reach 110 today. I'll roast in there."

"Would you rather die here?"

Snapping a set of handcuffs on Jake's wrists, Cindy stuffed a gag in his mouth. "If you're good, I'll let you out after I get the money."

When the trunk slammed over his head, Jake cursed his obstinacy. "Why don't I listen to my wife? If I survive this adventure, Samantha is going to kill me," he mused.

Jake thought he must have passed out. He certainly lost track of time in spite of his efforts to memorize the route Cindy was taking. After some minutes of what seemed to be highway driving, the car slowed down and the pattern switched to starts and stops. Finally, Cindy shut off the motor and Jake heard the car door slam. Ten minutes later, he was blinded by the bright daylight streaming through the opened trunk.

"Get those cuffs off of him and get him some water. Quick, he has been in there more than 40 minutes."

Blinking in the bright sunlight, Jake focused on his rescuers. Samantha was standing there with a bottle of water and a wet washcloth.

"Jake, you big lunk. If you had died I would've never forgiven myself. Are you alright?"

"I think so, I am a little cramped up and sore, and certainly hot and sweaty. Where's Cindy?"

It was Holly who answered. "We got her in custody. We wanted to wait until she actually got the money so we could catch her with it. Sorry Jake, that meant we had to wait to spring you from the trunk but Samantha said you would understand."

"I'll think about that, it was no fun being stuck in there. What was Cindy's haul?"

"Best guess, just having a quick look, at least 5 million maybe as much as 10 million."

"Wow. That was worth taking a risk for. But why did she need this key, where was the other."

Tom spoke up, "I can answer that, Jake. She was really clever, she mailed it to herself to be collected when she picked up her mail, but was worried about us having the Post Office staked out so she needed the spare key. We had gotten a court order, after Harry turned up dead, to open her mail. We found the key but had no idea which branch it was from. We were just going through the laborious process of tracking that down when Holly called this morning."

"Well, I'm glad you found me. How far back were you following?"

"We weren't, we were tracing your cell phone signal. Smart idea, Jake, to leave your phone on."

"It was Samantha's idea. She read it one of her detective novels. The good guys were able to trace the location of the call. We thought it might work as a backup."

om had a pained expression on his face. "It was more than a backup; we actually lost
e car for a while on visual tracking. She sprayed the stuff that obscures the plates and
hen she headed back toward Phoenix on 87, she actually passed our unit. We are going
 revise our training manual after this."

s they were joined by Deputy Lodestone, Holly said. "We're going to interrogate her
owntown. Want to sit in behind the one way glass and listen?"

Chapter Thirty Four

It was Jake and Samantha's first time to witness an interrogation in spite of having seen scores on TV and in the movies. The real thing was a bit of a letdown. Conducted by Holly and Tom, there was no intimidation or browbeating. Cindy seemed eager to tell her story and get it off her chest. What follows is the transcript of Cindy's confession as taken down by a stenographer and signed by Cindy Rousseau.

Cindy Rousseau's Statement
I don't know where to begin. It started about eighteen months ago. I was dancing at the Tropicana then. Harold, that is Harry Gianelli saw me there. He invited me to have dinner with him. He was funny and seemed to know a lot of people, people who might help me get out of the chorus line and into a starring role. At least, that's what he said. We quickly became intimate and carried on our affair for about a year. During that time he told me he was married but that the marriage was going downhill. His wife was a real fashion plate and spent his money like there was no tomorrow. She was a former model and liked fine clothes and expensive jewelry. She was always going to some charity function or other and, of course, needed something to wear.

She liked Harry's political connections and he wondered if she had married him to get into those circles. He said that seemed as important to her as the money he could provide. She spent a lot of time in elite social circles. After a while, Harry began to wonder if she was cheating on him, but she was real discreet. She flirted a lot, he could see, but always made a point of coming home with Harry. She kept a close chain on him Harry had a couple of old girl friends he'd been seeing before they were married and she made sure he ditched them after they tied the knot. If he so much as looked at a woman in that way, she lit into him about his wandering eye. Oh, I guess you are wondering how he got away with having an affair with me? Seemed she like she didn't care if he fooled around in Vegas. You know, 'what happens in Vegas, stays in Vegas.' But more important, it didn't affect her social standing in Chicago. In effect, he could screw around almost any place else, but not in their home town or anywhere he would be observed by her Gold Coast or North Shore friends.

She always made him use a rubber when they had sex. She told him she didn't want to get pregnant but most of all, she didn't want to catch anything he might have caught whoring around in Vegas and other places he took his political cronies. Carolyn knew he was unfaithful. It didn't bother her as long as it didn't interfere with her social standing. She also knew that sex was part of his 'business' of supplying politicians with a good time. Part of the bribes Harry arranged. That was what brought him to Vegas. He was always taking politicians there to gamble and get laid, as he put it. He was vulgar and crude. Carolyn didn't like that, Harry said, and neither did I. Sometimes I wonder why I put up with him.

But I did because he was my ticket out of the chorus line, or at least he seemed to be. He was always generous, giving me a few thousand dollars whenever I was with him. I know what you're thinking, I was just a high-priced call girl. But that's not true. I never irned tricks for money. I saw how those girls ended up. They would start at a thousand night and end up selling themselves for ten or twenty bucks. The smart ones put their noney away, but most spent it on drugs to dull their pain. That and buying clothes. It n't cheap being a high-priced hooker.

Jo, my relationship with Harry was different. What he gave me I used to pay my bills, et a better apartment and for papers for both of us to get away. At first it was just the ex and the promise of helping me move up. But after a couple of months, he started lling me his dreams of making a big score and getting away from Chicago. The Feds vere getting too close, uncovering sleaze balls in state government. Ryan, George Ryan, ne old governor was already in prison. Tony Rezko was on trial. Harry figured it was ast a matter of time before he got caught. Some developer he shook down or a politician vho ratted on him. He knew he was bound to be caught, his luck couldn't last. He was vorried about two things, going to prison or catching a slug from the mob. He knew he vas in danger and could be executed before he could turn state's evidence. The stakes vere high and he needed help getting away. He asked me to help him.

)o I love him? I don't know. I don't think so, but he was good to me and promised me a ot of money to help him. I figured I could bank my money, go with him to Mexico on ur fake IDs and when the fun ran out, come home. He figured he needed me to pass as is wife so he wouldn't look funny as a single guy crossing the border. He planned to eave some money in the States and needed someone he trusted to cross the border to get . He trusted me, said he was a genius in knowing who to trust.

o he would come to Vegas, and we would hook up. Most of the time he had politicians e was babysitting. Harry was real careful. He never introduced me to the men and vomen he brought. Yeah, he brought women too, not for sex, but because he was dealing vith them. Some were in government, some were business people. He told me Cook County has this rule that thirty percent of the county contracts have to go to businesses wned by minorities or women. Usually it's a slam dunk, but even then, some of the CEOs get taken on trips by Harry to jack up donations or as thanks for a big one. The crowd Harry brought to Vegas gambled and partied. He sometimes asked me to fix them up with dancers in the shows, men and women. I didn't like to pimp like that, but Harry and I were working on a bigger score and I never had to entertain any of his clients personally.

Harry kept it clean between me and his contacts. I was, like, isolated and insulated. Even when I pimped, I stayed away and never saw the contacts. My friends made out okay money wise and didn't complain. Harry spent as much time with me as he could and still entertain his guests. Once in a while he flew out alone when I got some time off and we drove to the Grand Canyon or some other sights just like normal people. It seemed like he was practicing how it would be like when he finally made his big score. He was fun to be with during those times, it was like we were normal, not like some criminals. We did try out the fake IDs on those trips to see if they would work. Sometimes on a three day trip we used three or four different names. Harry was careful. He had everything planned out.

I would ask him, 'How much are you gonna score, Harry?' He always answered, 'Enough, baby, enough.' He wouldn't tell me. Even when he came out, he didn't tell me. I only found out later how much he stole when I heard him quizzing Carolyn.

You probably think I was in it only for the money. Well, at first I was. But I started to care about Harry, or Harold as he was called in Scottsdale. But then I got to be afraid of him. I didn't feel I knew him anymore. He seemed to change. Maybe he was like that from the start, only out for himself. He really didn't care about me. He just used me. He needed someone to help him, I was as good as any, maybe better than most. He liked arm candy. Carolyn was a really good-looking woman. But he needed somebody smart who would do what he said and keep her mouth shut. Looking back, I see he was testing me, if I could follow instructions and keep quiet. Like when I got women for his contacts. Then when I got fake IDs and they weren't traceable back to Harry. These last few weeks I sometimes wondered if I would wind up like Carolyn, face bashed in and buried in some shallow grave when he was through with me. He is a selfish bastard. He can play a good game, but is only out for himself.

When everything was set up and we got the birth certificates of people about our age who had died, we were ready to skip the country, Harry slipped away from Chicago. He told Carolyn he was flying to New York on business. I hear she didn't give a damn, with all her charity balls to star at. Did I tell you he thought she was cheating on him when he was out of town? Here he was, working his political connections in Vegas and she was screwing one of her rich friends. Can you beat that! Anyway, he drove himself to O'Hare, or so he told her. He drove into long-term parking in case he was being followed. He didn't trust his mob friends, you see. After about twenty minutes, he paid his parking and drove out. He got on I-90 and starting making his way west. When he stopped, he used one of his fake IDs. At motels where they want a credit card, he gave them one of the cards we got, but then paid in the morning with cash so there were no charges to track. Harry's smart; he thinks of everything.

I met him in Vegas and we ditched his car at long term parking at the airport. Everything was ready to go and we took off for Phoenix. We lucked out with the rental. I'd been trying to get us a rental house but Harry was worried someone would track us. He was really pissed off at me and I saw for the first time what a temper he had. We dropped the agents I was using and just drove through the night to Phoenix. Next morning we started looking and by supper met Mrs. Bowden and rented her place starting the next week. We didn't have references but a couple of thousand under the table made her bite, plus all the rent in advance. We took off for a weekend in Sedona. Harry was edgy, I think from driving nearly straight through. Maybe being nervous about settling in Scottsdale   But he wanted an address for our passports to be sent to. The passport would be real, in fake names of course, but real US passports. He said we couldn't take a chance on using fake passports with all the checking since 9/11. That's why we were in Scottsdale...waiting for our passports. Then he up and disappears! I'll tell you more about that later. Whew, it's a relief to talk about all this!

Maybe you want to know how Carolyn found us. Well, when Harry's buddies found out he was missing, they went to his house. Carolyn said she didn't know where he was. She was roughed up a bit, they wanted to be sure she was telling the truth. After they figured out she really didn't know, they told her Harry had taken off with some of their money, a lot of their money. She did some quick checking and found out Harry cleaned out their bank account too, the thief! Then she saw her jewelry, which was worth a fortune, was missing from their safe deposit box. Usually they kept it in his home safe, but Harry insisted on renting a box 'cause someone was after him. To clinch it, he gave her a really nice necklace she's wanted. He told me it set him back 15 grand, but hell, he was looting her of jewelry that cost over three times that much so that was a net gain of 30 thousand. Actually, it was closer to $50 thousand, since he put the necklace on a credit card he had no plans to pay off! I hear she was really angry when she discovered what he'd done. His mob friends left her a number to call if Harry contacted her. She apparently called her husband every dirty name in the book. They suggested she and one of their trusted associates track him down.

Somehow through Harry's political cronies, his mob connections tracked me down. One of the politicians started an affair with a girl I fixed him up with. That's how they got to me. Harry, who could have bolted anywhere, had headed to Vegas. They told me that early on they thought he had headed for Canada. They figured he would cross the line some place where there was no border post in North Dakota or maybe Minnesota. But Harry figured they'd think that so he followed I-90. He even used his I-Pass to make them think he was going north. But after crossing into Wisconsin, tossed his I-Pass in a dumpster and doubled back through Iowa.

Harry knew he was well known in Vegas. That's why we met at long-term parking and transferred his stuff. He didn't want to be seen. But after the mob got my name, they tracked us to Arizona. We heard Willie the Cook had driven to take his arsenal of weapons with him. Harry told me he thought Willie was afraid of flying but I can't imagine that man being afraid of anything. Carolyn was such a seductive woman, she convinced Willie that after they caught up with Harry, they could take off for Europe with the money. Whether she meant it or not, we'll never know. But she and Willie were close, very close by the time they got to Arizona. They stopped in Vegas to pick up glamour photos of me and to interview my co-workers. I heard later that Willie roughed up the girl who finked on me to get her to talk. Willie didn't have the best manners. That's why I doubt Carolyn would've actually stuck with him. She was probably making it up as she went, trying to figure out how to stick it to Harry and also come out ahead herself. She was a real looker, and with enough money, she could start a new life somewhere else. A new life, that's what we all wanted.

Willie managed to track down the realtors who were looking for houses for me to rent. Harry was right to be angry about that. That was what gave them the tip we were headed for Phoenix. The mob also tracked down a couple of the guys I used to get fake IDs. They were persuaded to talk and tell them what names we were using. That's why we needed to find a new identity for Harry here in Phoenix. We used the regular way, going to a graveyard and finding the grave of someone who would be your age, but died as a

155

child. I was getting a new identity too, but it helped that I was using a stage name in Vegas and nobody they talked to knew my real name. By the way, my real name is Cindy Rousseau. So it was safe and easy to use that name. The realtors in Vegas only knew my stage name but recognized my photo. Ditto here in Phoenix, they used my photo to find the realtor that rented us our place. Fortunately the realtor played dumb an called me to warn me. I had said something about my new husband being on the run from a vicious and vindictive ex-wife. That was the same story I told Dr. Lowen when I asked him for help.

We laid low and got lucky, probably the only break we got. Harold spotted Carolyn coming out of a mall. I had to run in for something and when I came out, Harold was gone. He saw her get into Willie's car. The Illinois plates really stuck out. Harold followed them to a motel and saw their room number. By the time he came back to the mall to get me, he figured out a plan to try to get the drop on them. I was scared, really scared. But Harold needed me to drive one of the cars.

Late that night, Harold burst in on Willie and Carolyn. He emptied his pistol into Willie eight rounds. He had a silencer on his .45, it sounded like plop, plop, plop. He figured that he would catch Carolyn and Willie having sex and he was right. He thought he coulc shoot them both. The slugs went into Willie and missed her entirely. Willie toppled ove on her and she didn't have the chance to scream before Harold had a gag in her mouth and tied her up. Their room was on the first floor, the door right on the parking lot. We quickly cleaned up the room, stole the sheet on the bed which was blood stained and turned the mattress with the .45 slugs in it over. Actually, Harry told me later that there were only four bullet holes in the mattress, 'cause the other slugs stayed in Willie.

I was so freaked out I didn't know what to do. I just did what Harry told me to do. How managed to pack up their things, I will never know. I was working mechanically. All th while, Carolyn's eyes followed me around the room. I couldn't look at her. If I saw her eyes, all I could read in them was terror and pleading. I think she knew she was going to die. I don't know. I didn't know at that stage if Harry would kill me. I was just scared. When everything was packed up, Harry wiped our prints off everything. Actually, I thin he was wiping everyone's prints just to be sure. Willie was wrapped up in a bloody shee and blanket on the floor. Harry appreciated the arsenal that Willie was carrying with him; he felt that the guns would come in handy. Harry had a fascination with guns.

Checking the coast was clear, we dumped their bags in my car. Then Harry lugged Willie's body into the trunk of his car. He swiped a couple more blankets to keep any blood from seeping through. After he threw a coat over Carolyn's naked body, he forced her into the trunk with Willie's body. I think that's when she knew she was going to die. He sent me home and took off into the night in Willie's car. In the morning he came back and parked Willie's car in the garage. He still had Carolyn in the trunk but she had passed out. After he moved Willie's car into the garage, he got Carolyn out of the trunk and brought her around. He asked her about who was following him and what they knew. He particularly wanted to know if Willie had reported in to the outfit in Chicago. She claimed she talked Willie into running off with her when they recovered the money nd insisted he hadn't called in. Harry kept at it till he was sure she was telling the truth. She was tied naked to a chair in a dark room and at the end was whimpering. Harry wouldn't let me in the room but I could hear bits and pieces of the questioning. It gave me the creeps. I couldn't understand how he could be so cruel. It was then I realized there was a lot about Harry I didn't know. Finally, he strangled her with a stocking to not make marks. The whole thing made me sick, but what he did next really was more than I can take. He bashed in her face so no one would recognize her if they discovered her body before it decomposed. He was worried a body would not decompose fast enough. He even went to the public library to do internet research on how long it would take for a body to decompose in the desert. That night he drove to McDowell Sonoran Preserve and buried her in a shallow grave just off the trail. At least that's what he told me. He never told me what he did with Willie's body. I asked him and he told me I wouldn't want to know.

After that he was jumpy. He figured sooner or later someone would come looking for Willie. He got the idea to have me mail some cards from San Francisco to Carolyn's friends telling them that she was there on a vacation. I flew up from Phoenix in the morning and was back the same night. I drove all around making sure that there were several different postmarks on the cards. Harry said the writing was enough like hers to fool most people. Harry was a great one for figuring things out. He was always trying to stay not one step ahead but three or four. That's why I think he had a plan to get rid of me when he didn't need me anymore.

He got antsy sitting around the house. That's when he started going to the casino. He figured he was safe there, no one from Chicago would recognize him. When he couldn't gamble, he drank and got mean. I was really frightened for my life. I wanted out in the worst way.

We were almost ready to go, the passports, according the post office were due in a couple of weeks, but it could be longer with the passport backup. Harry didn't want to pay for expedited service because he was afraid it would call attention to the applications. He thought that the Feds couldn't check every application but might check the expedited ones.

Then Vinny Espennelli recognized him at the casino that night. Whether he recognized him from the back or saw him in the mirror, we'll never know. But Harold was throwing chips to the croupier and saw him in the mirror. Harold told me later that Vinny was never much of a poker player. His expression gave him away. Harold knew he had been made and Vinny would tell his brother Vitello. He hoped he wouldn't call him that night. With the time difference, probably he was safe. It was easy for me to call around to find what hotel they were staying at. I showed up at the desk in a trashy outfit and asked for Espennelli's room number. The desk clerk wouldn't give it out, but a $50 bill eased his tongue. I told him the man in the room hired me to entertain him and his wife, but I forgot the room number. When he offered to call the room, I told him that it was supposed to be a surprise for his wife and gave him a wink. Once we had the room number, we waited for the best time. There were too many people around that night.

Somebody down the hall was holding a party and it spilled out in the hallway. We would have been too conspicuous. When I saw their dinner tray, we figured or rather Harry figured that Vinny was too scared to go out to eat and ordered in. That probably would extend to breakfast and so Harry showed up early, knocked on the door and forced his way in. He took the wife as a shield, plugged Espennelli and then shot the wife.

He went straight to Sky Harbor and I met him there at the terminal and gave him a lift home. We dropped Willie's car and made it looked like Willie had made the hit and was on his way out of town. He was counting on the cops not knowing that Willie didn't like to fly.

After that he really laid low. He was watching from behind a curtain when Espennelli's brother showed up at your house. He thought about finishing off the wife but decided it was too risky. He wanted out and couldn't wait for the new passports to come. He was short tempered with me, but I knew I was safe, for a while at least.

The guy from the Airstream rental pulled up one day in our driveway. He had the house number wrong. He was just checking for connections before they delivered the trailer. I asked why they needed connections, he told me that a team were going to live in the trailer because a sick woman was going to stay with you. I asked who and that's when I got lucky. Turns out the guy is a crime news nut, follows all the stories. When Vitello Espennelli came to rent the trailer, the rental guy recognized the name. The rental guy didn't say anything to Espennelli but put two and two together.

That really shook up Harry. Not only was his botched hit coming back to haunt him, he was going to be living next door to Mrs. Espennelli and her bodyguards.

That was when we started making plans to clear out. I rented the car, parked it in the garage. Harry stole the plate off Bowden's car, we ditched his car at the airport and headed to the Grand Canyon. He wanted me to pick up the mail which we had put on hold and get our new passports. At least that's what he told me. He drugged me at the motel, took my money and left me stranded. That's the last time I saw the bastard.

I made my way back here to get the cash I stole from Harry and stashed away. I needed it to make a new start. I went into the house to retrieve the key but was jumped by somebody. Dr. Lowens' dog came to my rescue. I managed to get away but without the key. I hated to use Dr. Lowen that way and I'm really sorry for locking him in the trunk, but I was really scared and didn't know if I could trust anybody.

I know it was wrong to take the money, but you have to understand I was scared really badly. I should've gone to the police after he killed Willie and Carolyn but he told me I would be next if I even thought about ratting on him. I was pretty sure he would eventually kill me, but I didn't know what to do. That he trusted me enough to let me out of his sight to go shopping was probably an indication of how well I was able to act calm and on his side. I'm willing to testify against Harry for immunity from prosecution.

Chapter Thirty Five

olly came out of the interrogation room. "Well, what did you think? How did you like eeing your first interrogation? My thoughts are pretty clear but I want to hear yours rst."

I could spit nails! That woman is evil and feeding you a pack of lies. Arrest her on at ast one charge of murder, the murder of Harry Gianelli."

olly laughed, "I agree, Samantha, but let's hear your evidence. How are you so sure?"

Holly, that woman in there weaved truth with fiction to lead everyone astray. She retends she doesn't know Harry was killed. Big mistake, as it's been a hot news item on very station. She's cleverly planned and executed this scheme and is trying to bluff her ay out to the end."

But how would Cindy Rousseau be able to set up so elaborate of a scheme, she would eed to know so much about Chicago politics and the mob. I can't imagine Harry telling er that much in pillow talk." protested Jake.

Jake, I'm surprised at you! You were always telling your students not to trust verything they read on the internet, yet you fell for the same deception yourself."

What do you mean, Sam?"

You assumed the website you found on Cindy Rousseau was one that she had set up erself, but it wasn't. It was a clever plan, devised by Carolyn Gianelli, to cover up her wn disappearance. Carolyn set up the web site in Cindy Rousseau's name. The reason hat the close up photos of Carolyn looked like Cindy was because it was Carolyn's own hoto. She was creating an identity for Cindy Rousseau so that if you or anyone else hecked on Cindy, they would find Carolyn's photos and assume that they were looking t the real Cindy.

Remember how Cindy, that is Carolyn, told you that she had contacted rental agents in Las Vegas to find a house in Phoenix? That was true; the real Cindy had contacted ealtors in Vegas. But it was the fake Cindy that actually accompanied Harry or Harold as e was called to Phoenix to rent a home. That coincidence of our neighbor needing to ent her place furnished for six months was exactly what they were looking for. They eeded time to establish new identities and shift the money around so they could access t.

'Carolyn wanted Harry's money but not necessarily Harry, who eventually would attract ttention from his former associates, if not the Federal authorities investigating corruption n Illinois government. So she convinced Harry to find a woman in Vegas that looked like her, a double if you like. She didn't have to be an exact double, only close enough. Height and weight were the key issues, also hair color and skin tone. The plan from the beginning was to obliterate her facial features to delay identification, but the body type and coloring had to be correct. It probably took a while to find an unattached show girl, though a cocktail waitress would have done just as well. Ideally it would be a woman who had no permanent boyfriend, no family in the area and a girl Harry could influence. Maybe Carolyn accompanied Harry on one of his junkets, since he sometimes brought female contractors and women politicians. He wouldn't have needed to explain Carolyn's presence or perhaps she was in disguise. Who knows, she could have flown out earlier and met him clandestinely in Vegas. The point is Harry, with some help from Carolyn, found a woman who could stand in for her, so to speak. Harry romances the woman, gets her to buy him a car if she doesn't already own one, and starts setting things up. He bundles all his cash, drives out to Vegas, parks his car in a long term parking lot and joins up with the real Cindy Rousseau.

"At the appropriate interval, probably through some pre-arranged signal from Harry, Carolyn starts west, minded by Willie the Cook. Carolyn, before becoming a model, was an actress, who studied theater at DePaul University. I did some research on her myself and found this out through the Internet. She was actually quite good, but found she could make more money modeling and even more marrying Harry. Carolyn played the role of the wronged woman, abandoned by Harry. Willie, who had a weakness for women, was off his guard with Carolyn. She probably seduced him on the trip west which further unbalanced him. The story Cindy, as we knew her then, told about Willie being surprised by Harry has a ring of truth, though it's doubtful that Carolyn was anywhere near the line of fire. She may have drugged Willie; in any event, Willie was in no shape to resist Harry when Carolyn let him in the motel room. After Harry killed Willie, they dumped his body somewhere in the desert and poured lime over the body to add in decomposition Traces of lime were found in the trunk of Willie's car. It is probably true that Willie was naked when he was killed, all the easier to dispose of his clothes in a Good Will bin if there are no bullet holes in them.

"After killing Willie and disposing of his body, they drove to Phoenix in two cars, the one the real Cindy bought for Harry and Willie's car. It's probable Willie was killed somewhere between here and Vegas, but it could've been any place near to where they could dump the body without being seen. They rent a car in Phoenix and drive back to Vegas in one car, leaving the other parked in the garage. In Vegas, Harry links up with the real Cindy. He would have given her some story about flying in from Phoenix to explain why he didn't have a car. It's the easiest thing to be dropped at the airport by Carolyn and catch a cab to where Cindy was staying. Telling the real Cindy he had rented a place for them, they set out in Cindy's car. Somewhere between here and Vegas, Harry strangles Cindy and eventually buries her body in the shallow grave after obliterating her features. Why so near to where they are staying? That was a risk that they had to take. They needed to dispose of her in a place her body would be found and the wrong identification made. The reason they kept Willie's car was to throw everyone off the track. Willie or what is left of him is a couple of hundred of miles away. They would eventually leave his car somewhere to further throw off pursuit. When Vinny

160

cognized Harold, they used the situation to make it appear Willie Carlinski had made the hit on Vinny and Leila. Maybe they were both in on the hit; Carolyn in a maid's uniform knocking on the door with the tray, Harry pulling the trigger of the gun. Then they dump Willie's car in a very noticeable place to call attention to Willie as the shooter.

Then things got hot and it appeared that Harry's former associates were getting too close, the Rousseau's disappeared for a while. That was when Carolyn killed Harry and left his body in Tombstone. Again it was a way to throw everyone off the scent."

But apparently you weren't thrown off the scent," interjected Holly with a laugh, who up to this point, had been quietly listening.

No, not this bloodhound, my wife." inserted Jake. "But Sam, why did she come back? Why not clear off?"

It was for the money, Jake. They hadn't been able to get all the money or their new passports. She had asked the mail to be held, not forwarded and she needed to pick up the mail. She also needed help retrieving the rest of the money and that's when she conned you into being her assistant"

And you saved me before I met the same fate as Willie, Cindy, and Harold."

That's right. I love you, you big lunk, and I wasn't going to let some floozy do you in. I'm reserving that privilege for myself if you ever do me wrong!"

Made in the USA
Monee, IL
17 April 2023

31705639R00090